Joseph Jacobs, W. Frank Calderon

The Most Delectable History of Reynard the Fox

Joseph Jacobs, W. Frank Calderon

The Most Delectable History of Reynard the Fox

ISBN/EAN: 9783743400474

Manufactured in Europe, USA, Canada, Australia, Japa

Cover: Foto ©Andreas Hilbeck / pixelio.de

Manufactured and distributed by brebook publishing software (www.brebook.com)

Joseph Jacobs, W. Frank Calderon

The Most Delectable History of Reynard the Fox

THE
MOST DELECTABLE HISTORY

OF

REYNARD THE FOX

EDITED WITH INTRODUCTION AND NOTES

BY

JOSEPH JACOBS

DONE INTO PICTURES

BY

W. FRANK CALDERON

London

MACMILLAN AND CO.

AND NEW YORK

1895

PREFACE

NEXT to *Æsop*, *Reynard the Fox* is the best known of the tales in which animals play the chief part. It is natural, therefore, that a Cranford *Æsop* should be followed by a Cranford *Reynard;* and in the present volume I have endeavoured to do for *Reynard* what I attempted to do for *Æsop* in its predecessor—provide a text which children could read with ease and pleasure, and at the same time give their parents, their cousins, and their aunts a short *résumé* of the results which the latest research in folklore and literary history has arrived at with regard to the origin of the book.

With regard to the text, I found that ready-made to my hand. The late Sir Henry

Cole, of South Kensington fame, in his earlier days made an attempt to reform children's books, and may be regarded as the precursor of their improved position to-day. Under the name of " Felix Summerley " he produced a number of children's books, well printed, well written, and tolerably illustrated, which some of us remember as the chief treasures of our youth. Among these was a version of *Reynard*—mostly adapted from Caxton's—which I found, with some slight alteration, could easily be adapted for my present purpose, and, in the main, the text of the present book is a resuscitation of " Felix Summerley's " version.

As regards Introduction and Notes, I have attempted to give the adult reader a condensed account of the latest results about the origin of this interesting and characteristic product of the Middle Ages. Much has been done during the present century to clear up the many obscurities attaching to *Reynard the Fox*, which

shares with *Æsop* the distinction of being a
piece of folklore raised into literature.   I have
tried to summarise the results reached by such
authorities as Grimm, Voigt, Martin, and
Sudre, in their various monographs on the
subject.   For the present I confine myself to a
summary of their researches, as the small space
at my disposal prevents me entering into any
discussion of doubtful or controverted points.
I have for some time been engaged in a more
elaborate treatment of the subject, which will
ultimately appear in the *Bibliothèque de Carabas*
as a companion to my treatment of *Æsop* in
the same series.   I owe it to the courtesy of
Mr. Nutt that I am able to deal with it in a
more popular manner before the publication of
the results of my own research.   For the
present I confine myself to a summary of the
researches of others.

JOSEPH JACOBS.

INTRODUCTION

Raginhard was once a man's name, tolerably widely spread, both in Germany itself and in the Debatable Land between France and Germany which forms at once both the link and the bone of contention between the two countries. It is composed of two Teutonic roots, one of which is represented by our English *hard*, and the other which exists only in the Gothic *ragin*, with the sense of 'counsel.' Raginhard thus means 'strong in counsel,' and, therefore, is well adapted for the name of the beast which, most of all animals, lives by its wits. In a slightly modified form it has become in French the only name by which the fox is known, the earlier form *goupil* having become replaced by *renard*, owing to the widespread popularity of the Beast Satire in which the fox plays so prominent a part.

These philological facts are of somewhat

INTRODUCTION

RAGINHARD was once a man's name, tolerably widely spread, both in Germany itself and in the Debatable Land between France and Germany which forms at once both the link and the bone of contention between the two countries. It is composed of two Teutonic roots, one of which is represented by our English *hard*, and the other which exists only in the Gothic *ragin*, with the sense of ' counsel.' Raginhard thus means ' strong in counsel,' and, therefore, is well adapted for the name of the beast which, most of all animals, lives by its wits. In a slightly modified form it has become in French the only name by which the fox is known, the earlier form *goupil* having become replaced by *renard*, owing to the widespread popularity of the Beast Satire in which the fox plays so prominent a part.

These philological facts are of somewhat

more significance than the usual barren inquiry into the derivation of words. They lead us at once into most of the points of interest or dispute with which scholarly inquiry has concerned itself about Reynard the Fox. The relative importance of France and Germany, of the Celtic and the Teutonic genius, in originating the Satire, the significance of a proper name being attached to an animal species, the distinction between the Fable and the Beast Satire, the popularity of the latter among the Folk, and its relation to the Folk-tales dealing with the same subject—all these topics are suggested by the mere consideration of the name of our hero. German and French scholars have, naturally, much to say upon a topic in which Germany and France are equally interested, and there can be no doubt that at times patriotic zeal has attempted to supply the place of historic fact. Yet that very zeal has served its purpose, for when competent scholars fall out Truth comes by her own.

Let us dismiss out of our way the more certainly attested facts relating to the early literary history of Reynard. Like most of the favourite medieval productions of the Romantic Period, versions of it occur in the chief languages of Western Europe. There is the German *Reinhart*, dated by modern scholarship *circa* 1180. There is the French *Roman de Renard*, with its twenty-six or seven 'branches,' to the nucleus of which a provisional date of 1230 may be assigned, though many of the 'branches' are earlier and some later. There is the Flemish *Reinaert*, the earliest part of which was composed by a certain Willem, near Ghent, about 1250. While there is beyond these a Latin poem, *Ysengrimus*, written at Ghent in 1148. Even in England a trace has been found of a metrical version of the Satire in the form of a thirteenth-century poem, entitled, *Of the Vox and of the Wolf*. Of the Italian *Rainardo*, and of the medieval Greek version, there is no occasion to speak, since they are out of the running in the race for priority.

The results summed up in a few words above are the outcome of a long series of critical investigations by German, French, and Dutch scholars, started by the monograph of Jacob Grimm on *Reinhart Fuchs* in 1824. He originated the theory that Reynard was the outcome of an ancient Teutonic Beast Epic of primitive origin. Every step in the investigation since his time has tended to strip his theory of every vestige of plausibility, and it may be now regarded as having gone the way of all exploded theories.   All the versions referred to above are of literary origin, and with the exception of the *Ysengrimus*, that origin, even the Germanists allow, is French. Both the *Reinhart* and the *Reinaert* are derived from French originals, now lost, which have been revised and extended to form the *Roman de Renard*. The whole family is thus derived from a French parent, who flourished somewhere between 1150 to 1170, though it is from a Flemish descendant that all modern versions, including Caxton's and Goethe's, and the one represented in the book before us, have been derived.

But though we can trace our book to a literary original, it does not follow that it is entirely or solely literary in origin. Man has been defined as a tale-telling animal; it comes as natural to him to tell tales as to cook food. Thus, a tale may arise naturally among the Folk, even though it must ultimately be written down by somebody who can write. One is, naturally, inclined to suspect a Folk origin for tales like those contained in *Æsop's Fables*, or

Reynard the Fox, which represent animals act-
ing and talking with all the duplicity of men.
Accordingly, it is the tendency of recent research to attempt to discover how far and in
what way certain Folk fables were worked up
by the literary artist of the eleventh century, who
was the father of the family of the Reynards.

The question is complicated in various
ways.   Many incidents of the Reynard are
mere modifications of Æsopic fable, and might
be only literary renderings of those popular
tales.   Thus, Voigt has traced all the incidents
of the Latin *Ysengrimus*, the firstborn of all the
Reynard family now in existence, to literary
sources, whether Æsop, or the *Physiologus*, or to
Peter Alfonsi.   But the very medium in which
it is composed proves that the *Ysengrimus* is a
learned monkish product, and it is not, therefore, strange that it should have an entirely
literary origin.   No such origin, however, can
be claimed for many of the incidents common
to the Reynard in its popular German, French,
and Flemish forms.   To take a striking
example, the stratagem by which the Fox
induces the Wolf to fish with his tail through
a hole in the ice occurs nowhere in literature
before the Reynard, and unless actually in-

vented by the author must have been found among the Folk.

It is found among the Folk, even to the present day, that incident of the Iced Wolf's Tail. Dr. Krohn, a Finnish savant, has found no less than a hundred and seventy-one variants of the incident collected by folklorists in all the four quarters of the globe. Still, nearly all of these have been printed this century, and it remains possible that they have been derived, directly or indirectly, from the Reynard itself. But though possible, this is far from being probable. It is little likely, for example, that the Finns, among whom no less than ninety-eight variants of the incident have been discovered, were at any time diligent students of Reynard, nor can we attribute similar learning to Uncle Remus, who also tells the tale. No, we must assume that the Iced Wolf's Tail has lived among the Folk for over a thousand years, and that it was from the Folk that the French satirist first adopted it.

Some, indeed, would go further, and contend that it has lived among the Folk in all places where it is found, because it is natural to the Folk to think of wolves or bears fishing with their tails in the ice. But by going further in this particular instance they certainly fare worse. For the story has spread into lands where there is no ice at all, and where, accordingly, it could not have arisen independently. If it could have spread to these lands, there is no reason to suppose that it could not have spread to lands favoured with ice in the winter. All we need assume for the present purpose is that it either originated in, or spread to, North-Eastern France in the twelfth century, and was there taken up by the original author of *Reynard* into his fable.

What he did with the Iced Wolf's Tail he must have done with other incidents of the Cycle which are not found in earlier literary sources, but which are found among the Folk of to-day. In my Notes on the various incidents given in the book before us, I have pointed out which were probably derived from Fable Literature, and which from the Folk. One of the chief points of interest in the study of the Reynard is this mixture of literature and folk-lore which thus gave rise to a new form of literature. Investigation of this mixture has been begun by the capable hands of M. Sudre, but the investigation is by no means at an end.

So much for the present on the origin of

the book.   But the question of origins is far from being the only one which it raises.   The very form in which the tale is told is original. The fable speaks of the Lion, the Wolf, or the Fox.   The Reynard talks of Noble, of Isengrim, or of Reynard.   The type is individualised and made personal.   The artistic gain of such a procedure is clear, and is proved, above all, by the fact that the personal name of the Fox has, in France at least, replaced the name of the species.   One might have thought, at first sight, that this individualising process had been performed by the literary artist to whom we owe the Reynard.   But there is a curious piece of evidence proving that the Wolf at least received such an individualised name before any literary form of the Reynard had come into existence.   In 1112 a tumult arose at Laon, during which the life of the Bishop Gaudri came into danger, and he concealed himself in a cask.   Among his pursuers was one Teudegald, whom the Bishop had been accustomed to call Isengrim, on account of his wolf-like appearance.   'For so,' adds the chronicler, 'some are wont to call wolves.' When Teudegald came near the cask he tapped it and called out, 'Is Isengrim at home?'

and so had his revenge for the Bishop's insult. Both Gaudri and Teudegald were clearly familiar with the name of Isengrim, which was, therefore, current among the Folk before the rise of the Reynard Cycle.

From a comparison of the earliest forms M. Gaston Paris, than whom no more competent authority can be cited, comes to the conclusion that among the animals which had individualised names from the first, were Reynard the Fox, Bruin the Bear, Baldwin the Ass, Belier the Ram, Tibert the Cat, Hirsent the Lady Wolf, Richut the Vixen. All these names are German in origin, and might seem at first sight to stand in the way of the French contention for a French origin to the Cycle. Not at all, answer M. Paulin Paris, and his son, German names were quite common among the Franks, and need not surprise us among the French. When pressed for details they are able to find these personal names in cartularies of the eleventh and twelfth centuries. They are, however, obliged to recognise the fact that some of these names are only to be found in documents relating to Lorraine, and it is, accordingly, in this district that we must seek for the origin of the names of the Cycle.

Whether we are to call Lorraine French or
German depends on which side of the Rhine
we were born.   From this side of the Channel
one feels inclined to 'hedge' and call the
names Franco-Teutonic.

Another set of names in the Cycle are of
interest, because they are appellative and not
personal.   Noble the Lion, Chanticleer the
Cock, Kyward the Hare derive their names
from their qualities, and imply an allegorising
tendency in those who acted as their godfathers.
These names increase in the latter development
of the fable, and thus afford the crucial test
of the relative antiquity of the various branches.
Thus, the earliest of them, as represented by
the German *Reinhart*, contains only one such
appellative name, Chanticleer, and that in such
a form that it was clearly not appellative to the
German writer.   It is owing to the significance
and critical importance of these names that I
have devoted such attention to them in the
annotations to this volume.

The increasing tendency to give significant
names to the various beasts introduced marks
a change that came over the Reynard after the
earlier stages of its development.   When the
beasts had only personal names given to them

their adventures were told by the Folk, as the adventures of persons are told, for the purpose of raising a laugh.　Later on when significant names were given to the new beast personages introduced, there was a meaning, and often a bitter meaning, underlying the laugh.　The Beast Jest had grown into the Beast Satire. The story of the adventures of Sir Wolf and Sir Fox, told first merely to raise a guffaw, became in the hands of the later developers of the thesis means of casting ridicule on the institutions of Medieval Society.　The hypocrisy of the Monk, the greed of the Noble, the craft of the Lawyer, the conquest of the world by cunning wickedness—these were the themes which formed the *farrago* of the later branches of the Reynard Cycle.　While seemingly only continuing the earlier adventures of their beast heroes, a change had come over the spirit of the Cycle : the Beast Epic had become a World Satire.

The earlier critics of Reynard laid almost exclusive stress upon this satiric aspect of the Cycle.　The *Roman de Renard* was regarded as an outcome of the same literary movement that produced the second and satiric half of the *Roman de la Rose*.　Carlyle, in the remarks on

Reynard, which he included in his essay on *Early German Literature*, regarded it almost solely from this point of view.

'A true Irony must have dwelt in the Poet's heart and head. Here, under grotesque shadows, he gives us the sadder picture of Reality; yet for us without Sadness; his figures mask themselves in uncouth bestial vizards, and enact gambolling; their Tragedy dissolves into sardonic grins.'

The progress of critical research has shown that Carlyle was mistaken in regarding Irony as the original motive force for the Reynard Cycle, which came in later in the French developments of it in consonance with the satiric tendencies of the Gallic genius. But in its inception the Reynard was a Beast Comedy rather than a Beast Satire. The Comedy came from the Folk, the Satire from the Literary Artist. The closest analogy is offered by those modern redressings of folk-tales like Thackeray's *Rose and Ring*, or Mr. Lang's *Prince Prigio*, worthy pendant to that other, in which the modern literary artist uses the Folk form in which to express his genial Satire.

Reverting for a moment to the form in which the earlier adventures of Reynard are found among the Folk we are enabled to guess with some precision, owing to the researches of M. Sudre, the set of tales on which the twelfth-century artist based his work. The outrage of Reynard on Dame Wolf, the Iced Wolf's Tail, the Fishes in the Car, the Bear in the Cleft, the Wolf as Bell-ringer, the Dyed Fox, together with the Æsopic Fables of the Sick Lion, the Lion's Share, the Fox and the Goat, and the Fox, Cock, and Dog—these form the chief Folk ingredients out of which the artist of the Reynard made up his tale. But how ingeniously did he weld them into an artistic whole! In his hands the insult offered by the Fox to Dame Wolf becomes the starting-point of a whole Beast Epic, dealing with the feud between the Fox and the Wolf, which, ultimately, draws in all the other animals in its train, till the court of King Noble becomes like Verona in the days of the Montagues and the Capulets.

Curiously enough, Dr. Krohn has found these Folk incidents of the Cycle scattered separately among the Folk in all parts of the world. Still more curiously he finds all these incidents, and more also, current among the Finnish folk even at the present day.[1] He connects eleven incidents into a Folk History of the feud of the Wolf and the Fox, constituting a definite chain of tradition, each link of which is bound up inextricably with all the rest. Here, then, it would seem we have found among the Finnish folk of to-day the actual Beast Epic which the French artist of the twelfth century dressed up with his own adornments seven centuries ago. But closer investigation robs this thesis of most of its plausibility. The chain does not occur in Finland as a chain, but in separate links, so that the epic character of the so-called chain at once disappears. Many of the links, indeed, occur, as some of my readers may remember, in the tales collected from Uncle Remus by Mr. J. C. Harris, so that it is impossible to regard the existence of an original Folk Epic as substantiated by Dr. Krohn's ingenious researches.

The interest of those researches lies in a different direction. M. Sudre's researches have shown that in the eleventh and twelfth centuries a series of folk-tales existed dealing

[1] K. Krohn, *Die geografische Verbreitung einer modischen Thiermärchenkette in Finnland.* In *Fennia*, organ of the Helsingfors Literary Society, vol. iv. pt. 4.

with the enmity of the Fox and the Wolf, or, as some say, of the Fox and the Bear. Dr. Krohn has shown that precisely these traditions still exist as traditions among the Folk of to-day. We have, accordingly, evidence here of the continued existence of a fable among the Folk for at least seven centuries, during which it has spread through all the continents.

M. Sudre and Dr. Krohn go even further. They think they can localise the original home and scene of at least one part of the tradition. The incident of the Iced Wolf's Tail, to which I have already referred, occurs in many places, especially in North Europe, as the Iced Bear's Tail, and is there used to explain why the Bear's tail is so short. It is, indeed, obvious, that the story as told in the Reynard Cycle loses much of its efficacy from the fact that the Wolf is nearly as well provided with a brush as Master Reynard himself. The Reynard story can only be told of an individual Wolf, the Northern folk-tale is appropriately applied to the Bear in general. If we regard the Northern Fable as the original, it is, in its way, a myth told to explain a natural phenomenon, viz. 'Why the Bear's tail is so short,' the actual title of one of the folk-tales.

Here, then, we seem to be getting back to the position of Grimm, that for at least one part of the Reynard Cycle there is a mythological source current among the Northern European nations. But even this modicum of Grimm's position is rendered doubtful, as has been shown by M. Gaston Paris, by the fact that even the Northern nations are not unanimous in keeping to the Bear. It is more probable that the mythological explanation was added when the Bear was substituted for the Wolf, than that the mythology was dropped when Isengrim took the place of the Bear. We are, accordingly, reduced to the conclusion that in this case the Great Bear does not point to the Pole.

But after all, these investigations and theories as to the origin, meaning, and source of the Reynard have little bearing upon the attraction it had for our forefathers, and to a more limited extent for ourselves. Amid the complexities of life it is an obvious convenience to possess a means by which its problems can be presented in simpler terms. The Fable or the Allegory is primarily intended to simplify the problem in this way. The Fable, in particular, does this by identifying the elementary virtues and vices with the characters of the best known birds, beasts, and fishes. Man may be the most interesting thing to man, but animals are more interesting to children and to men of childlike mind. The cynic has observed, ' The more I know of men, the more I respect dogs.' But the fabulists invert the process and say that the more they observe animals the more they understand men. What applies to the simpler fable is even more applicable to the more elaborate Beast Satire, which is better suited to display the complicated forces which go to make up life.

The life depicted in the Reynard is, indeed, a somewhat limited one. We have got down to ' hard pan,' as American miners say. It is, in truth, the bare struggle for existence that Reynard portrays, and is a fit outcome of the Feudal Age when for all but the barons life was but a bare struggle. Medieval literature presents us, for the most part, pictures of life as seen by those above the salt. Reynard, the Fabliaux, and Villon present us with life as it appeared to the Disinherited Folk. What a life is there presented! Greed, hypocrisy, brute force, and cunning rule the roast. Force

and cunning are the only two powers re-
cognised, and if the book has a moral, it is
merely the low one that cunning is more
powerful than force.

But it is scarcely the Moral, or the Allegory,
which has attracted so many to *Reynard the
Fox*.   It is the adventurous, shifty, eponymous
Hero who captures our interest.   We have
all a sneaking regard for the crafty villain who
can control Circumstance, even though we salve
our conscience by the implicit thought, ' But
for the grace of God, there go I.'   There
is something artistic in the way the villain
moulds Circumstance to his own ends which
extorts our reluctant admiration.   His career
is a long series of making fools of his enemy,
and to the primitive mind the ' sell ' is the most
exquisite form of practical wit.

To the medieval mind · the triumphs of
Reynard were even more attractive than they
can be nowadays.   When brute force un-
blushingly ruled the world cunning was your
only remedy against the tyrant.   Every district
in those days had its Noble, its Isengrim, and
its Bruin, and all the villagers who suffered
from their cruelty felt a sympathetic interest
in the triumphs of Reynard over them.   Theo-

retically the Hero ought to represent our best self; if Reynard in some ways represented the worst, the medieval conditions of life were mainly to blame.

There is another source of interest to which Reynard appealed, and still appeals. Mr. Vincent Crummles knew the human heart when he placed upon the Portsmouth stage a hero of five feet nothing combating successfully with three antagonists, all of larger inches. 'Go it, little un' is the natural cry in an unequal battle of this description, and Reynard, in his multifarious intrigues against Noble, Isengrim, and Bruin, enlists our sympathy much as David or Jack the Giant-killer has us on his side in the conflict with the Giant.

Reynard had another source of attraction in the Middle Ages and at the time of the Reformation. At times he manages to gain his ends by donning a monk's cowl. He confesses his sins, and is scarcely absolved before he longs to repeat them. He thus became a type of the hypocrisy of the monkish nature. A good deal of his popularity in Germany has been due to his Protestant proclivities. Earlier investigators were inclined to lay overmuch stress on this side of the Reynard.   Writing was, in great measure, a monopoly of the monks in the Middle Ages, and there was, accordingly, evidence that most versions of the Reynard were written down, if not composed, by monks. This made the whole Cycle seem to be a confession of weakness by the monks. But more dispassionate inquiry has shown that the satiric attack upon monkery is a later development, and cannot be in any sense regarded as a primary *motif* in the Cycle. Yet it adds many a quaint passage in the later forms of the book, and cannot be disregarded in any treatment of the subject, however cursory.

Enough has now been said to put the reader in a position where he can best begin the reading of Reynard. He has to expect a novel of adventure in which animals play the part of men, and for the most part bear men's names. The traits of character he will be called upon to observe will be mainly those which men can be supposed to share with beasts. Through it all he will see Cunning clad in Fox pelt extricating itself against invincible odds out of the most desperate difficulties. Fables he knows of in the ancient world he will find repeated under novel circumstances; while other fables, possibly as old as those, have been rescued by the Medieval Satirist from the Folk and woven cunningly into the narrative. And amidst it all he will remember that, while the story-teller was relating the shifts by which Reynard overcame Noble, Isengrim, and Bruin, he was, as often as not, pointing the sly finger of scorn at the Lawyer, the Squire, or the Parson of the Parish.

CONTENTS

CHAPTER V

CHAPTER VI

CHAPTER VII

CHAPTER VIII

CHAPTER IX

CHAPTER X

CHAPTER XI

CHAPTER XII

How Reynard *made his Confession before the King*

CHAPTER XIII

How Reynard *the Fox was honoured of all beasts by the King's* commandment

CHAPTER XIV

How Isegrim *and his wife* Ereswine *had their shoes plucked off, for* Reynard *to wear to* Rome

CHAPTER XV

How Kyward *the Hare was slain by* Reynard *the Fox, and sent by the Ram to the King* .

CHAPTER XVI

How Bellin *the Ram and his lineage were given to the Bear and the Wolf*

CHAPTER XVII

How the King was angry at these complaints, took counsel for revenge, and how Reynard *was forewarned by* Grimbard *the Brock* .

CHAPTER XVIII

CHAPTER XIX

CHAPTER XX

CHAPTER XXI

CHAPTER XXII

CHAPTER XXIII

CONTENTS

CHAPTER XXIV

CHAPTER XXV

CHAPTER I

How the Lion *proclaimed a solemn Feast at his Court, and how* Isegrim *the Wolf and his Wife, and* Curtois *the Hound, made their first complaints of* Reynard *the Fox.*

It was about the Feast of *Pentecost* (which is commonly called Whitsuntide), when the woods are in their lusty-hood and gallantry, and every tree clothed in the green and white livery of glorious leaves and sweet-smelling blossoms, and the earth is covered in her fairest mantle of flowers, while the birds with much joy entertain her with the delight of their harmonious songs. Even at this time and entrance of the lusty spring, the *Lion*, the royal King of beasts, to celebrate this holy feast time with all triumphant ceremony, intends to keep open court at his great palace of *Sanden*, and to that end, by solemn proclamation, makes known over all his kingdom to all beasts whatsoever, that, upon pain to be held in contempt, every one should resort to that great celebration. Within a few days after, at the time appointed, all beasts both great and small came in infinite multitudes to the court, only *Reynard* the fox excepted, who knew himself guilty in so many trespasses against many beasts, that his coming thither must needs have put his life in great hazard and danger.

Now when the King had assembled all his court together, there were few beasts found but made their several complaints against the fox, but especially *Isegrim* the wolf, who, being the first and principal complainant, came with all his lineage and kindred, and standing before the King, spoke in this manner:

‘My dread and dearest Sovereign Lord the King, I humbly beseech you, that from the height and strength of your great power, and the multitude of your mercies, you will be pleased to take pity on the great trespasses and unsufferable injuries which that unworthy creature *Reynard* the fox hath done to me, my wife, and our whole family. Now to give your highness some taste of these, first know (if it please your Majesty) that this *Reynard* came into my house by violence, and against the will of my wife, where, finding my children laid in their quiet couch, he there assaulted them in such a manner that they became blind. For this offence a day was set and appointed wherein *Reynard* should come to excuse himself, and to take a solemn oath that he was guiltless of that high injury; but as soon as the book was tendered before him, he that well knew his own guiltiness refused to swear, and ran instantly into his hole, both in contempt of your Majesty and your laws. This, my dread Lord, many of the noblest beasts know which now are resident in your court: nor hath this alone bounded his malice, but in many other things he hath trespassed against me, which to relate, neither the time nor your highness's patience would give sufferance thereunto. Suffice it, mine injuries are so great that none can exceed them, and the shame and villainy he hath done to my wife is such that I can neither bide nor suffer it unrevenged, but I must expect from him amends, and from your Majesty mercy.'

When the wolf had spoken these words, there stood by him a little hound whose name was *Curtois*, who, stepping forth, made likewise a grievous complaint unto the King against the fox, saying that in the extreme cold season of the winter, when the frost was most violent, he being half starved and detained from all manner of prey, had no more meat left him to

sustain his life than one poor pudding; which pudding the said *Reynard* had most unjustly taken away from him.

But the hound could hardly let these words fly from his lips, when, with a fiery and angry countenance, in sprang *Tibert* the cat amongst them, and falling down before the King, said, 'My Lord the King, I must confess the fox is here grievously complained upon, yet were other beasts' actions searched, each would have enough to do for his own clearing. Touching the complaint of *Curtois* the hound, it was an offence committed many years ago, and though I myself complain of no injury, yet was the pudding mine and not his; for I won it by night out of a mill when the miller lay asleep, so that if *Curtois* could challenge any share thereof, it must be from mine interest.'

When *Panther* heard these words of the cat, he stood forth and said, 'Do you imagine, *Tibert*, that it were a just or a good course that *Reynard* should not be complained upon? Why the whole world knows he is a murderer, a vagabond, and a thief.   Indeed he loveth not

truly any creature, no not his Majesty himself, but would suffer his highness to lose both honour and renown, so that he might thereby attain to himself but so much as the leg of a fat hen; I shall tell you what I saw him do yesterday to *Kyward* the hare, that now standeth in the King's protection.   He promised unto *Kyward* that he would teach him his *credo*, and make him a good chaplain; he made him come sit between his legs and sing and cry aloud *credo, credo*. My way lay thereby, and I heard the song: then coming nearer, I found that Mr. *Reynard* had left his first note and song, and begun to play his old

deceit; for he had caught *Kyward* by the throat, and had I not come at that time, he had taken his life also, as you may see by the fresh wound on *Kyward* at this present. O my Lord the King, if you suffer this unpunished, and let him go quit, that hath thus broken your peace, and profaned your dignity, and doing no right according to the judgment

of your laws, your princely children many years
hereafter shall bear the slander of this evil.'

'Certainly, *Panther*,' said *Isegrim*, 'you
say true, and it is fit they receive the benefit
of justice that desire to live in peace.'

CHAPTER II

How Grimbard *the Brock spake for* Reynard *before*
the King.

THEN spake *Grimbard* the brock, that was
Reynard's sister's son, being much moved with
anger : '*Isegrim*, you are malicious, and it is a
common saw, *Malice never spake well ;* what can
you say against my kinsman *Reynard ?* I would
you durst adventure, that whichever of you had
most injured one another might die the death,
and be hanged as a felon. I tell you, were he
here in the court, and as much in the King's
favour as you are, it would be much too little
satisfaction for you to ask him mercy. You
have many times bitten and torn my kinsman
with your venomous teeth, and oftener much
than I can reckon, yet some I will call up to
my remembrance.

'Have you forgot how you cheated him
with the plaice which he threw down from the

cart, when you followed aloof for fear? Yet you devoured the good plaice alone, and gave him no more but the great bones which you could not eat yourself. The like you did with the fat flitch of bacon, whose taste was so good, that yourself alone did eat it up, and when my uncle asked his part, you answered him with scorn, "Fair young man, thou shalt have thy share." But he got not anything, albeit he won the bacon with great fear and hazard, for the owner came, and caught my kinsman in a sack, from whence he hardly escaped with life. Many of these injuries hath *Isegrim* done to *Reynard*, which I beseech your lordships judge if they be sufferable.

'Now comes *Kyward* the hare with his complaint, which to me seems but a trifle, for if he will learn to read, and read not his lesson aright, who will blame the schoolmaster *Reynard* if he give him due correction? for if scholars be not beaten and chastened they will never learn.

'Lastly complaineth *Curtois* that he with great pain had gotten a pudding in the winter, being a season in which victuals are hard to find; methinks silence would have become him better, for he had stolen it ; and *Male quæ-sisti, et male perdidisti*—that is to say, it is fit that be evil lost which was evil won ; who can blame *Reynard* to take stolen goods from a thief?   It is reason that he which understands the law and can discern right, being of great and high birth as my kinsman is, do right unto the law.   Nay, had he hanged up *Curtois* when he took him with the manner, he had offended none but the King in doing justice without leave ; wherefore, for respect to his Majesty, he did it not, though he reaped little thanks for his labour.   Alas, how do these complaints hurt him! mine uncle is a gentleman and a true man, nor can he endure falsehood ; he doth nothing without the counsel of his priest.   I affirm, since my Lord the King proclaimed his peace, he never thought to hurt any man.   He eateth but once a day, he liveth as a recluse, he chastiseth his body, and weareth a shirt of haircloth ; it is above a year since he ate any flesh (as I have been truly informed by them which came but yesterday from him) ; he hath forsaken his castle *Malepardus*, and abandoned all royal state, a poor hermitage retains him, hunting he hath forsworn, and his wealth he hath scattered, living only by alms and good men's charities; doing infinite penance for his sins, so that he is become pale and lean with praying and fasting.'

Thus, whilst *Grimbard* his nephew stood preaching, they perceived coming down the hill unto them, stout *Chanticleer* the cock, who brought upon a bier a dead hen, of whom *Reynard* had bitten off the head, and was brought to the King to have knowledge thereof.

CHAPTER III

How Chanticleer *the Cock complained of* Reynard *the Fox.*

CHANTICLEER marched foremost, smote piteously his hands and feathers, whilst on the other side the bier went two sorrowful hens—the one was *Tantart*, the other the good hen *Cragant*, being two of the fairest hens between *Holland* and *Arden;* these hens bore each of them a straight bright burning taper, and these hens were sisters to *Copple*, which lay dead on the bier, and in the marching they cried piteously, ' Alack and well-a-day for the death of *Copple*, our dear sister.' Two young hens bare the bier, which cackled so heavily, and wept so loud for the death of *Copple* their mother, that the hills gave an echo to their clamour. Thus being come before the King, *Chanticleer*, kneeling down, spake in this manner:

' Most merciful and my great Lord the

King, vouchsafe, I beseech you, to hear our complaint, and redress those injuries which *Reynard* hath unjustly done to me, and to my children that here stand weeping.   For so it is, most mighty sir, that in the beginning of April,

when the weather was fair, I being then in the height of my pride and glory, because of the great stock and lineage I came of, and also I had eight valiant sons, and seven fair daughters, which my wife had hatched, all which were strong and fat, and walked in a yard well walled and fenced round about, wherein they had in several sheds for their guard six stout mastiff dogs, which had torn the skins of many wild beasts, so that my children feared not any evil which might happen unto them. But *Reynard*, that false and dissembling traitor, envying their happy fortune because of their safety, many times assailed the walls, and gave such dangerous assaults, that the dogs divers times were let forth unto him and hunted him away. Yea, once they lighted upon him, and bit him, and made him pay the price for his theft, and his torn skin witnessed; yet nevertheless he escaped, the more was the pity; albeit, we were quit of his troubling a great while after. At last he came in the likeness of a hermit, and brought me a letter to read, sealed with your Majesty's seal, in which I found written, that your highness had made peace throughout all your realm, and that no manner of beast or fowl should do injury one to another. He affirmed unto me that for his own part he was become a monk or cloistered recluse, vowing to perform a daily penance for his sins; and showed unto me his beads, his books, and the hair shirt next to his skin, saying in humble wise unto me, "Sir *Chanticleer*, never henceforth be afraid of me, for I have vowed never-

more to eat flesh. I am now waxed old, and would only remember my soul; therefore I take my leave, for I have yet my noon and my even song to say." Which spake, he departed, saying his *credo* as he went, and laid him down under a hawthorn; at this I was exceeding glad, that I took no heed, but went and clucked my children together, and walked

without the wall, which I shall ever rue. For false *Reynard*, lying under a bush, came creeping betwixt us and the gate, and suddenly surprised one of my children, which he trussed up in his mail and bore away, to my great sorrow. For having tasted the sweetness of our flesh, neither hunter nor hound can protect or keep him from us. Night and day he waits upon us with that greediness, that of fifteen of my children he hath left me but four unslaughtered, and yesterday *Copple* my daughter, which here lieth dead on this bier, was after her murder, by a kennel of hounds, rescued from him. This is my plaint, and this I leave to your highness's mercy to take pity of me, and the loss of my fair children.'

CHAPTER IV

The King's answer to the Cock's *complaint, and how they sung the* Dirge.

THEN spake the King: 'Sir *Grimbard*, hear you this of your uncle the recluse? he hath fasted and prayed well; and well, believe me, if I live a year, he shall dearly abide it. As for you, *Chanticleer*, your complaint is heard and shall be cured; to your daughter that is dead, we will give her the right of burial, and with solemn dirges bring her to the earth, with worship; which finished, we will consult with our lords how to do you right and justice against the murderer.' Then began the *Placebo Domine*, with all the verses belonging to it, which are too many to recite; and as soon as the dirge was done, the body was interred, and upon it a fair marble stone laid, being polished as bright as glass, in which was engraven in great letters this inscription following:

**Copple,
Chanticleer's daughter,
whom Reynard the fox hath slain,
lieth here buried;
Mourn thou that readest it,
for her death was unjust and lamentable.**

After this the King sent for his lords and wisest counsellors to consult how this foul murder of *Reynard's* might be punished. In the end it was concluded that *Reynard* should be sent for, and without all excuse to appear before the King to answer those trespasses should be objected against him, and that this message should be delivered by *Bruin* the bear. To all this the King gave consent, and calling him before him, said, 'Sir *Bruin*, it is our pleasure that you deliver this message, yet in the delivery thereof have great regard to yourself, for *Reynard* is full of policy, and knoweth how to dissemble, flatter, and betray. He hath a world of snares to entangle you withal, and without great exercise of judgment, will make a scorn and mock of the best wisdom breathing.'

'My Lord,' answered Sir *Bruin*, 'let me alone with *Reynard*, I am not such a truant in

discretion, to become a mock to his knavery ;'
and thus full of jollity the bear departed ; if his
return be as jovial, there is no fear in his well
speeding.

CHAPTER V

How Bruin *the Bear sped with* Reynard *the Fox.*

THE next morning away went *Bruin* the bear in quest of the fox, armed against all plots of deceit whatsoever. And as he came through a dark forest, in which *Reynard* had a bypath, which he used when he was hunted, he saw a high mountain, over which he must pass to go to *Malepardus*. For though *Reynard* have many houses, yet *Malepardus* is his chiefest and most ancient castle, and in it he lay both for defence and ease. Now at last when *Bruin* was come to *Malepardus*, he found the gates close shut, at which after he had knocked, sitting on his tail, he called aloud, 'Sir *Reynard*, are you at home? I am *Bruin* your kinsman, whom the King hath sent to summon you to the court, to answer many foul accusations exhibited against you, and hath taken a great vow, that if you fail to appear to this summons, that your life

shall answer your contempt, and your goods
and honours shall lie confiscate at his highness's
mercy.   Therefore, fair kinsman, be advised of
your friend, and go with me to the court to
shun the danger that else will fall upon you.'

Reynard, lying close by the gate, as his
custom was for the warm sun's sake, hearing

those words, departed into one of his holes, for
Malepardus is full of many intricate and curious
rooms, which labyrinth-wise he could pass
through, when either his danger or the benefit
of any prey required the same.   There he medi-
tated awhile with himself how he might
counterplot and bring the bear to disgrace
(whom he knew loved him not) and himself to
honour; at last he came forth, and said, ' Dear
uncle *Bruin*, you are exceeding welcome;

pardon my slowness in coming, for at your first speech I was saying my even song, and devotion must not be neglected. Believe me, he hath done you no good service, nor do I thank him which hath sent you this weary and long journey, in which your much sweat and toil far exceeds the worth of the labour. Certainly had you not come, I had to-morrow been at the court of my own accord, yet at this time my sorrow is much lessened, inasmuch as your counsel at this present may return me double benefit. Alas, cousin, could his Majesty find no meaner a messenger than your noble self to employ in these trivial affairs? Truly it appears strange to me, especially since, next his royal self, you are of greatest renown both in blood and riches. For my part, I would we were both at court, for I fear our journey will be exceeding troublesome. To speak truth, since I made mine abstinence from flesh, I have eaten such strange new meats, that my body is very much distempered, and swelleth as if it would break.'

'Alas, dear cousin,' said the bear, 'what meat is that which maketh you so ill?'

'Uncle,' answered he, 'what will it profit you to know? the meat was simple and mean. We

poor men are no lords, you know, but eat that
for necessity which others eat for wantonness,
yet not to delay you, that which I ate was
honeycombs, great, full, and most pleasant,
which, compelled by hunger, I ate too un-
measurably and am thereby infinitely distempered.'

'Ha,' quoth *Bruin*, 'honeycombs? do you
make such slight respect of them, nephew?
why it is meat for the greatest emperor in the
world. Fair nephew, help me but to some of
that honey, and command me whilst I live; for
one little part thereof I will be your servant
everlastingly.'

'Sure,' said the fox, 'uncle, you but jest with
me.'

'But jest with you,' replied *Bruin;* 'beshrew
my heart then, for I am in that serious earnest,
that for one lick thereat you shall make me the
faithfullest of all your kindred.'

'Nay,' said the fox, 'if you be in earnest,
then know I will bring you where so much is,
that ten of you shall not be able to devour it at
a meal, only for your love's sake, which above
all things I desire, uncle.'

'Not ten of us?' said the bear, 'it is impossible; for had I all the honey betwixt *Hybla*

and *Portugal,* yet I could in a short space eat it all myself.'

'Then know, uncle,' quoth the fox, 'that near at hand here dwelleth a husbandman named *Lanfert,* who is master of so much honey, that you cannot consume it in seven years,

which for your love and friendship's sake I will put into your safe possession.'

Bruin, mad upon the honey, swore, that to have one good meal thereof he would not only be his faithful friend, but also stop the mouths of all his adversaries.

Reynard, smiling at his easy belief, said, 'If you will have seven ton, uncle, you shall have it.'

These words pleased the bear so well, and made him so pleasant, that he could not stand for laughing.

Well, thought the fox, this is good fortune, sure I will lead him where he shall laugh more measurably; and then said, 'Uncle, we must delay no time, and I will spare no pain

for your sake, which for none of my kin I would perform.'

The bear gave him many thanks, and so away they went, the fox promising him as much honey as he could bear, but meant as many strokes as he could undergo. In the end they came to *Lanfert's* house, the sight whereof made the bear rejoice. This *Lanfert* was a stout and lusty carpenter, who the other day had brought into his yard a great oak, which, as their manner is, he began to cleave, and had struck into it two wedges in such wise that the cleft stood a great way open, at which the fox rejoiced much, for it was answerable to his wish. So with a laughing countenance he said to the bear, 'Behold now, dear uncle, and be careful of yourself, for within this tree is so much honey that it is unmeasurable. Try if you can get into it, yet, good uncle, eat moderately, for albeit the combs are sweet and good, yet a surfeit is dangerous, and may be troublesome to your body, which I would not for a world, since no harm can come to you but must be my dishonour.'

'Sorrow not for me, nephew *Reynard*,' said the bear, 'nor think me such a fool that I cannot temper mine appetite.'

'It is true, my best uncle, I was too bold. I pray you enter in at the end, and you shall find your desire.'

The bear with all haste entered the tree, with his two feet forward, and thrust his head into the cleft, quite over the ears, which when the fox perceived, he instantly ran and pulled the wedges out of the tree, so that

he locked the bear fast therein, and then neither flattery nor anger availed the bear. For the nephew had by his deceit brought the uncle into so false a prison that it was impossible by any art to free himself of the same. Alas, what profited now his great strength and valour? Why they were both causes of more vexation; and finding himself

destitute of all relief, he began to howl and bray, and with scratching and tumbling to make such a noise, that *Lanfert*, amazed, came hastily out of his house, having in his hand a sharp hook, whilst the bear lay wallowing and roaring within the tree.

The fox from afar off said to the bear in scorn and mocking, 'Is the honey good, uncle, which you eat? How do you? Eat not too much, I beseech you. Pleasant things are apt to surfeit, and you may hinder your journey to the court. When *Lanfert* cometh (if your belly be full) he will give you drink to digest it, and wash it down your throat.'

And having thus said, he went towards his castle. But by this time, *Lanfert*, finding the bear fast taken in the tree, he ran to his neighbours and desired them to come into his yard, for there was a bear fast taken there. This was noised through all the town, so that there was neither man, nor woman, nor child but ran thither, some with one weapon, and some with another—as goads, rakes, broom-staves, or what they could gather up. The priest had the handle of the cross, the clerk the holy water sprinkler, and the priest's wife, Dame *Jullock*, with her distaff, for she was then spinning ; nay, the old beldames came that had ne'er a tooth in their heads. This army put *Bruin* into a great fear, being none but himself to withstand them, and hearing the clamour of the noise which came thundering upon him, he wrestled and pulled so extremely, that he got out his head, but he left behind him all the skin, and his ears also ; insomuch that never creature beheld a fouler or more deformed beast. For the blood covering all his face, and his hands leaving the claws and skin behind them, nothing remained but ugliness. It was an ill market the bear came to, for he lost both motion and sight— that is, feet and eyes. But notwithstanding this torment, *Lanfert*, the priest, and the whole parish came upon him, and so be-cudgelled him about his body part, that it might well be a warning to all his misery, to know that ever the weakest shall still go most to the wall. This the bear found by experience, for every one exercised the height of their fury upon him. Even *Houghlin* with the crooked leg, and *Ludolf* with the long broad nose, the one with a leaden mall, and the other with an iron whip, all belashed poor sir *Bruin*, not so much but sir *Bertolf* with the long fingers, *Lanfert* and *Ortam* did him more annoyance than all the rest, the one having a sharp Welsh hook, the other a crooked staff well leaded at the end, which he used to play at stab ball withal. There was *Birkin* and *Armes Ablequack*, *Banc* the priest with his staff, and Dame *Jullock* his wife; all these so belaboured the bear, that his life was in great danger. The poor bear in this massacre sat and sighed extremely, groaning under the burden of their strokes, of which *Lanfert's* were the greatest and thundered most dreadfully; for Dame *Podge* of *Casport* was his mother, and his father was *Marob* the steeple-maker, a passing stout man when he was alone. *Bruin* received of him many showers of stones till *Lanfert's* brother, rushing before the rest with a staff, struck the bear in the head such a blow, that he could neither hear nor see, so that awaking from his astonishment the bear leaped into the river adjoining, through a cluster of wives there standing together, of which he threw divers into the water, which was large and deep, amongst whom the parson's wife was one; which the parson seeing how she floated like a sea-mew, he left striking the bear, and cried to the rest of the company, 'Help! oh help! Dame *Jullock* is in the water; help, both men and women, for whosoever saves her, I give free pardon of all their sins and transgressions, and remit all penance imposed whatsoever.' This heard, every one left the bear to help Dame *Jullock*, which as soon as the bear saw, he cut the stream and swam away as fast as he could, but the priest with a great noise pursued him, crying in his rage, 'Turn, villain, that I may be revenged of thee;' but the bear swam in the strength of the stream and suspected not his calling, for he was proud that he was so escaped from them. Only he bitterly cursed the honey tree and the fox, which had not only betrayed him, but had made him lose his hood from his face, and his gloves from his fingers. In this sort he swam some three miles down the water, in which time he grew so weary that he went on land to get ease, where blood trickled down his face; he groaned, sighed, and drew his breath so short, as if his last hour had been expiring.

Now whilst these things were in doing, the fox in his way home stole a fat hen, and threw her into his mail, and running through a bypath that no man might perceive him, he came towards the river with infinite joy; for he suspected that the bear was certainly slain: therefore said to himself, 'My fortune is as I wished it, for the greatest enemy I had in the court is now dead, nor can any man suspect me guilty thereof.' But as he spake these words, looking towards the river, he espied where *Bruin* the bear lay and rested, which struck his heart with grief, and he railed against *Lanfert* the carpenter, saying, 'Silly fool that thou art, what madman would have lost such good venison, especially being so fat and wholesome, and for which he took no pains, for he was taken to his hand; any man would have been proud of the fortune which thou neglectest.' Thus fretting and chiding, he came to the river, where he found the bear all wounded and bloody, of which *Reynard* was only guilty; yet in scorn he said to the bear, '*Monsieur, Dieu vous garde.*'

'O thou foul red villain,' said the bear to himself, 'what impudence is like to this?'

But the fox went on with his speech, and said, 'What, uncle? have you forgot anything at *Lanfert's*, or have you paid him for the honeycombs you stole? If you have not, it will redound much to your disgrace, which before you shall undergo, I will pay him for them myself. Sure the honey was excellent good, and I know much more of the same price. Good uncle, tell me before I go, into what order do you mean to enter, that you wear this new-fashioned hood? Will you be a monk, an abbot, or a friar? Surely he that shaved your crown hath cropped your ears; also your foretop is lost, and your gloves are gone; fie, sloven, go not bare-handed, they say you can sing *peccavi* rarely.'

These taunts made *Bruin* mad with rage, but because he could not take revenge, he was content to let him talk his pleasure. Then after a small rest he plunged again

into the river, and swam down the stream,
and landed on the other side, where he began
with much grief to meditate how he might
get to the court, for he had lost his ears, his
talons, and all the skin off his feet, so that
had a thousand deaths followed him, he could
not go. Yet of necessity he must move,
that in the end compelled by extremity, he
set his tail on the ground, and tumbled his
body over and over, so by degrees, tumbling
now half a mile, and then half a mile, in the
end he tumbled to the court, where divers
beholding his strange manner of approach,
they thought some prodigy had come towards
them ; but in the end the King knew him,
and grew angry, saying, 'It is sir *Bruin*,
my servant ; what villains have wounded him
thus, or where hath he been that he brings
his death thus along with him ? '

'O my dread Sovereign Lord the King,'
cried out the bear, 'I complain me grievously
unto you ; behold how I am massacred,
which I humbly beseech you revenge on
that false *Reynard*, who, for doing your royal
pleasure, hath brought me to this disgrace
and slaughter.'

Then said the King, 'How durst he do

this? now by my crown I swear I will take the revenge which shall make the traitors tremble!'

Whereupon the King sent for all his council, and consulted how and in what sort to persecute against the fox, where it was generally concluded that he should be again summoned to appear and answer his trespasses; and the party to summon him they appointed to be *Tibert* the cat, as well for his gravity as wisdom; all which pleased the King well.

CHAPTER VI

How the King sent Tibert *the Cat for* Reynard *the*
Fox.

THEN the King called for sir *Tibert* the cat,
and said to him, 'Sir *Tibert*, you shall go to
Reynard, and say to him the second time, and
command him to appear, and answer his
offences; for though he be cruel to other
beasts, yet to you he is courteous. Assure
him if he fail at your first summons, that I will
take so severe a course against him and his
posterity, that his example shall terrify all
offenders.'

Then said *Tibert* the cat, 'My dread Lord,
they were my foes which thus advised you, for
there is nothing in me that can force him either
to come or tarry. I beseech your Majesty
send some one of greater power; I am little
and feeble. Besides, if noble sir *Bruin*, that
is so strong and mighty, could not enforce him,
what will my weakness avail?'

The King replied, 'It is your wisdom, sir *Tibert*, I employ, and not your strength, and many prevail with art, when violence returns with lost labour.'

'Well,' said the cat, 'since it is your pleasure, it must be accomplished; Heaven make my fortune better than my heart presageth.'

This *Tibert* made things in readiness, and went towards *Malepardus*, and in his journey he saw come flying towards him one of Saint *Martin's* birds, to whom the cat cried aloud, 'Hail, gentle bird, I beseech thee turn thy wings and fly on my right hand.' But the bird turned the contrary way, and flew on his left side; then grew the cat very heavy, for he was wise and skilful in augurism, and knew the sign to be ominous; nevertheless, as many do, he armed himself with better hope, and went to *Malepardus*, where he found the fox standing before his castle gates, to whom *Tibert* said, 'Health to my fair cousin *Reynard*, so it is that the King by me summons you to the court, in which if you fail or defer time, there is nothing more assured unto you than a cruel and a sudden death.'

The fox answered, 'Welcome, dear cousin

Tibert, I obey your command, and wish my Lord the King infinite days of happiness, only let me entreat you to rest with me to-night, and take such cheer as my simple house affordeth. To-morrow, as early as you will, we will go towards the court, for I have no kinsman I trust so dearly as yourself. Here was with me the other day the treacherous knight sir *Bruin* the bear, who looked upon me with that tyrannous cruelty, that I would not for the wealth of an empire have hazarded my person with him. But, my dear cousin, with you I will go, were a thousand sicknesses upon me.'

Tibert replied, 'You speak like a noble gentleman, and methinks it is best now to go forward, for the moon shines as bright as day.'

'Nay, dear cousin,' said the fox, 'let us take the day before us, so may we encounter with our friends; the night is full of danger and suspicion.'

'Well,' said the cat, 'if it be your pleasure, I am content, what shall we eat?'

Reynard said, 'Truly my store is small, the best I have is a honeycomb, too pleasant and sweet, what think you of it?"

Tibert replieth, 'It is meat I little respect.

and seldom eat; I had rather have one mouse than all the honey in *Europe*.'

'A mouse,' said *Reynard*, 'why, my dear cousin, here dwelleth a priest hard by, who hath a barn by his house so full of mice that I think half the wains in the parish are not able to bear them.'

'O dear *Reynard*,' quoth the cat, 'do but lead me thither, and make me your servant for ever.'

'Why,' said the fox, 'love you mice so exceedingly?'

'Beyond expression,' quoth the cat; 'why, a mouse is beyond venison or the delicatest cates on princes' tables; therefore conduct me thither, and command my friendship in any matter; had you slain my father, my mother, and all my kin, I would clearly forgive you.'

CHAPTER VII

How Tibert *the Cat was deceived by* Reynard *the*
Fox.

THEN said *Reynard*, ' Sure you do but jest.'

' No, by my life,' said the cat.

' Well, then,' quoth the fox, ' if you be in earnest, I will so work that this night I will fill your belly.'

' It is not possible,' said the cat.

' Then follow me,' said the fox, ' for I will bring you to the place presently.'

Thus away they went with all speed to the priest's barn, which was well walled about with a mud wall, where but the night before the fox had broken in, and stolen from the priest an exceeding fat hen, at which the priest was so angry, that he had set a gin or snare before the hole to catch him at his next coming, which the false fox knew perfectly, and therefore said to the cat, ' Sir *Tibert*, creep in at this hole, and believe it you shall not tarry a minute's

space, but you shall have more mice than you
are able to devour.   Hark, you may hear how
they peep; when your belly is full, come again,
and I will stay and await for you here at
this hole, that to-morrow we may go together
to the court.   But, good cousin, stay not too
long, for I know my wife will hourly expect us.'

'Then,' said the cat, 'think you I may
safely enter in at this hole? these priests are
wise, and subtle, and couch their danger so
close, that rashness is soon overtaken.'

'Why, cousin *Tibert*,' said the fox, 'I
never saw you turn coward before; what, man,
fear you a shadow?'

The cat, ashamed at his fear, sprang quickly
in at the hole, but was presently caught fast

by the neck in the gin, which as soon as the cat felt and perceived, he quickly leaped back again, so that the snare running close together, he was half strangled, so that he began to struggle and cry out and exclaim most piteously.

Reynard stood before the hole and heard all, at which he infinitely rejoiced, and in great scorn said, 'Cousin *Tibert*, love you mice? I hope they be well fed for your sake; knew the priest or Martinet of your feasting, I know them of so good disposition, they would bring you sauce quickly. Methinks you sing at your meat, is that the court fashion? If it be, I would *Isegrim* the wolf were coupled with you, that all my friends might be feasted together.'

But all this while the poor cat was fast, and mewed so piteously, that Martinet leaped out of bed, and cried to his people, 'Arise, for the thief is taken that had stolen our hens.'

With these words the priest unfortunately rose up and awaked all in his house, crying, 'The fox is taken, the fox is taken!' and arising, he gave to *Jullock* his wife an offering candle to light, and then coming first to *Tibert*, he smote him with a great staff, and after him many other, so that the cat received many deadly blows, and the anger of Martinet was so great, that he struck out one of the cat's eyes, which he did to second the priest, thinking at one blow to dash out the cat's brains. But the cat perceiving his death so near him, in a desperate mood he leaped upon the priest, and scratched and tore him in so dread a manner, that the poor priest fell down in a swoon, so that every man left the cat to revive the priest. And whilst they were doing this, the fox returned home to *Malepardus*, for he imagined the cat was past all hope to escape. But the poor cat seeing all his foes busy about the priest, he presently began to gnaw and bite the cord, till he had sheared it quite asunder in the midst. And he leaped out of the hole and went roaring and stumbling, like the bear, to the King's court. But before he got thither, it was fair day, and the sun being risen, he entered the court like the pitifullest beast that ever was beheld; for by the fox's craft his body was beaten and bruised, his bones shivered and broken, one of his eyes lost, and his skin rent and mangled.

This when the King beheld, and saw *Tibert* so pitifully mangled, he grew infinitely angry and took counsel once more how to revenge the injuries upon the fox. After some con-sultation, *Grimbard* the brock, *Reynard's* sister's son, said to the rest of the King's council, ' My good lords, though my uncle were twice so evil as those complaints make him, yet there is remedy enough against his mischiefs. There-

fore it is fit you do him justice as to a man of his rank, which is, he must be the third time summoned, and if then he appear not, make him guilty of all that is laid against him.'

Then the King demanded of the brock whom he thought fittest to summon him, or who would be so desperate to hazard his hands, his ears, nay, his life, with so tyrannous and irreligious a being?

'Truly,' answered the brock, 'if it please your Majesty, I am that desperate person who dare adventure to carry the message to my most subtle kinsman, if your highness but command me.'

CHAPTER VIII

How Grimbard *the Brock was sent to bid the Fox to the Court.*

THEN said the King, 'Go, *Grimbard*, for I command you; yet take heed of *Reynard*, for he is subtle and malicious.'

The brock thanked his Majesty, and so taking humble leave, went to *Malepardus*, where he found *Reynard* and *Ermelin* his wife sporting with their young whelps; then having saluted his uncle and his aunt, he said, 'Take heed, fair uncle, that your absence from the court add not more mischief to your cause than the offence doth deserve. Believe, it is high time you appear at the court, since your delay doth beget but more danger and punishment. The complaints against you are infinite, and this is your third time of summons; therefore your wisdom may tell you, that if you delay but one day further, there is not left to you or yours any hope of mercy. For within three

days your castle will be demolished, your
kindred made slaves, and yourself exempted
for a public example. Therefore, my best
uncle, I beseech you recollect your wisdom,
and go with me presently to the court, I doubt
not but your discretion shall excuse you, for
you have passed through many as eminent
perils, and made your foes ashamed, whilst the
innocence of your cause hath borne you spot-
less from the tribunal.'

Reynard answered, ' Nephew, you say true,
and I will be advised and go with you, not to
answer offences, but in that I know the court
stands in need of my counsel. The King's
mercy I doubt not, if I may come to speak with
his Majesty, though mine offences were ten
times doubled; for I know the court cannot
stand without me, and that shall his highness
understand truly. Though I know I have
many enemies, yet it troubles me not; for mine
innocence shall awaken their injuries, and they
shall know that in high matters of state and
policy *Reynard* cannot be missing. They may
well harp upon things, but the pitch and
ground must come from my relation. It is the
envy of others hath made me leave the court,
for though I know their shallowness cannot

disgrace me, yet may their multitudes oppress me; nevertheless, nephew, I will go with you to the court, and answer for myself, and not hazard the welfare of my wife and children. The King is too mighty, and though he do me injury, yet will I bear it with patience.' This spoke, he turned to his wife and said, ' Dame *Ermelin*, have care of my children, especially *Reynardine* my youngest son, for he had much of my love, and I hope will follow my steps; also *Rossel* is passing hopeful, and I love them entirely, therefore regard them, and if I escape, doubt not but my love shall requite you.'

At this leave-taking *Ermelin* wept, and her children howled, for their lord and victualler was gone, and *Malepardus* left unprovided.

CHAPTER IX

How Reynard *shrove him to* Grimbard *the Brock*.

WHEN *Reynard* and *Grimbard* had gone a good way on their journey, *Reynard* stayed and said, 'Dear nephew, blame me not if my heart be full of care, for my life is in great hazard, yet to blot out my sins by repentance, and to cast off the burthen, give me leave to shrive myself unto you. I know you are holy, and having received penance for my sin, my soul will be at quiet.'

Grimbard bade him proceed; then said the fox, '*Confitebor tibi pater*.'

'Nay,' said the brock, 'if you will shrive you to me, do it in English, that I may understand you.'

Then said *Reynard*, 'I have grievously offended against all the beasts that live, and especially mine uncle, *Bruin* the bear, whom I lately massacred; then *Tibert* the cat, whom I ensnared in a gin. I have trespassed against

Chanticleer and his children, and have devoured many of them; nay, the King hath not been quiet of my malice, for I have slandered him and his Queen. I have betrayed *Isegrim* the wolf, and called him uncle, though no part of his blood ran in my veins; I made him a monk of *Elmare*, where I became also one of the order only to do him open mischief. I made him bind his feet to a bell-rope to teach him to ring, but the peal had like to have cost him his life, the men of the parish beat and wounded him so sore. After this I taught him to catch fish, but he was soundly beaten therefore, and feeleth the stripes at this instant. I led him to steal bacon at a rich priest's house, where he fed so extremely, that not being able to get out where he got in, I raised all the town upon him, and then went where the priest was set at meat, with a fat hen before him; which hen I snatched away, so that the priest cried out, " Kill the fox, for never man saw thing so strange, so that the fox should come into my house, and take my meat from before me. This is a boldness beyond knowledge." And with these words he threw his knife at me, but he missed me, and I ran away, whilst he pursued me crying, " Kill the fox, kill the fox," and after him a world of people, whom I led to the place where *Isegrim* was, and there I let the hen fall, for it was too heavy for me (yet much against my will), and then springing through a hole, I got into safety. Now as the priest took up the hen, he espied *Isegrim*, and then cried out, " Strike, friends, strike, here is the wolf, by no means let him escape." Then the people ran all together with clubs and staves, and with a dreadful noise, giving the poor wolf many a deadly blow, and some throwing stones after him, hit him such mortal blows on the body that the wolf fell down as if he had been dead, which perceived, they took him and dragged him by the heels over stocks and stones, and in the end threw him into a ditch without the village, and there he lay all night, but how he got thence I know not. Another time I led him to a place where I told him were seven hens and a cock, set on a perch, all lusty and fat, and hard by the place stood a fall door, on which we climbed; then I told him if he would creep in at the door he should find the hens. Then *Isegrim* with much joy went laughing to the door, and entering in a little, and groping about, he said, "*Reynard*, you abuse me, for here is nothing." Then replied I,

" Uncle, they are farther, and if you will have them, you must adventure for them; those which used to sit there I myself had long since." At this the wolf going a little farther, I gave him a push forward, so that he fell down in the vault, and his fall was so great, and made such a noise, that they which were asleep in the house awaked and cried that something was fallen down at the trap-door; whereupon they arose and lighted a candle, and espying him, they beat and wounded him to death. Thus I brought the wolf to many hazards of his life, more than I can now either remember or reckon, which as they come to my mind I will reveal to you hereafter.

' Thus have I told you my wickedness, now order my penance as shall seem fit in your discretion.'

Grimbard was both learned and wise, and therefore brake a rod from a tree, and said, ' Nephew, you shall three times strike your body with this rod, and then lay it down upon the ground, and spring three times over it without bowing your legs or stumbling. Then shall you take it up and kiss it gently in sign of meekness and obedience to your penance; which done, you are absolved of your sins committed this day, for I pronounce unto you clear remission.'   At this the fox was exceeding

glad, and then *Grimbard* said unto him, 'See that henceforth, uncle, you do good works, read your Psalter, go to church, fast vigils,

keep holy days, give alms, and leave your sinful and evil life, your theft, and your treason, and then no doubt you shall attain mercy.'

The fox promised to perform all this, and so they went together towards the court; but a little beside the way as they went, stood a religious house of nuns, where many geese, hens, and capons went without the wall; and as they went talking, the fox led *Grimbard* out of his right way to that place. And finding the poultry walking without the barn, amongst which was a fat young capon, which strayed a little from his fellows, he suddenly leaped at and caught him by the feathers, which flew about his ears, but the capon escaped, which *Grimbard* seeing, said, 'Accursed man, what will you do, will you for a silly pullet fall again into all your sins? mischief itself would not do it.'

To which *Reynard* answered, 'Pardon me, dear nephew, I had forgotten myself, but I will ask forgiveness, and mine eye shall no more wander'; and then they turned over a little bridge; but the fox still glanced his eye toward the poultry, and could by no means refrain it, for the ill that was bred in his bones still stuck to his flesh, and his mind carried his

eyes that way as long as he could see them ;
which the brock noting, said, ' Fie, dissembling
cousin, why wander your eyes so after the
poultry ? '

The fox replied, ' Nephew, you do me injury so to mistake me, for mine eyes wandered

not, but I was saying a *paternoster* for the souls
of all the poultry and geese which I have slain
and betrayed, in which devotion you hindered
me.'

' Well,' said *Grimbard*, ' it may be so, but
your glances are suspicious.'

Now by this time they were come into

the way again, and made haste towards the court, which as soon as the fox saw, his heart quaked for fear; for he knew well the crimes he was to answer, that they were infinite and heinous.

CHAPTER X

*How the Fox came to the Court, and how he excused
himself.*

As soon as it was bruited in the court that
Reynard the fox, and *Grimbard* his kinsman
were arrived there, every one, from the highest
to the lowest, prepared himself to complain of
the fox; at which *Reynard's* heart quaked, but
his countenance kept the old garb, and he went
as proudly as ever he was wont with his nephew
through the high street, and came as gallantly
into the court as if he had been the King's son
and as clear from trespass as the most innocent
whosoever; and when he came before the chair
of state, in which the King sat, he said,
' Heaven give your Majesty glory and renown
above all the princes of the earth; I assure
your highness there was never king had a truer
servant than myself have been to you, and yet
am, and so will die. Nevertheless, my dread
Lord, I know there be many in this court that

seek my confusion, if they could win belief with your Majesty.   But you scorn the slanders of malice, and although in these days flatterers have the most room in princes' courts, yet with you it is not so, nor shall they reap anything but shame for their labour.'

But the King cut him short at these words, and said, 'Peace, traitorous *Reynard*, I know your dissimulation, and can expound your flattery, but both shall now fail you. Think you I can be caught with the music of your words? No, it hath too oft deceived me; the peace which I commanded and swore unto, that have you broken.'

And as he would have gone forward, *Chanticleer* crying out, 'O how have I lost this noble peace?'

'Be still, *Chanticleer*,' said the King, and then he proceeded, 'Thou evil among good ones, with what face canst thou say thou lovest me, and seest all those wretched creatures ready to disprove thee, whose very wounds yet spit bloody defiance upon thee; and for which believe thy dearest life shall answer.'

'*In nomine patris, etc.*,' said the fox, 'my dread Lord, if *Bruin's* crown be bloody, what is that to me? If your Majesty employed him

F

in a message, and he would neglect it to steal
honey at the carpenter's house, where he received his wounds, how shall I amend it? If
revenge he sought, why did he not take it
himself, he is strong and puissant? As for
Tibert, whom I received with all friendship, if
he against my will or advice will steal into the
priest's barn to catch mice, and there lose his
eyes, nay, his life, wherein is mine offence, or
how become I their guardian? O my dread
Lord, you may do your royal pleasure, and
however mine innocence plead, yet your will
may adjudge me to what death contents you.
I am your vassal, and have no support but your
mercy; I know your strength and mine own
weakness, and that my death can yield you but
small satisfaction, yet whatsoever your will is,
that to me shall be most acceptable.'

And as he thus spake, *Bellin* the ram
stepped forth, and his ewe dame *Oleway*, and
besought the King to hear their complaint;
with them *Bruin* the bear and all his mighty
lineage; and *Tibert* the cat, *Isegrim* the wolf,
Kyward the hare, and *Panther*, the boar, the
camel, and *Bruel* the goose, the kid and the
colt, *Baldwin* the ass, *Bortle* the bull, and
Hamel the ox, the weasel, *Chanticleer* the

cock, and *Partlet* with all her children ; all
these with one entire noise cried out against
the fox, and so moved the King with their
complaints, that the fox was taken and
arrested.

CHAPTER XI

How the Fox was arrested and judged to death.

UPON this arrest a parliament was called, and every voice went that *Reynard* should be executed. Notwithstanding he answered every objection severally, though great art was used both in one and the other, to the wonderful admiration of all that heard him. But witnesses examined, and every proof made pregnant, the fox was condemned, and judgment was given, that he should be hanged till his body were dead; at which sentence the fox cast down his head, for all his jollity was lost, and no flattery nor no words now prevailed.

This done, *Grimbard* his nephew, and divers others near him in blood (which could not endure to see him die) took their leave of the King and departed from the court. When the King noted what gallant young gentlemen departed thence, all sad and weeping, being near of the fox's blood and alliance, he said to himself, ' It behoveth us to take good and mature counsel; though *Reynard* have some faults, yet he hath many friends, and more virtues.'

As the King was thus thinking, the cat said to the bear, ' Sir *Bruin*, and you, sir *Isegrim*, why are you slow in this execution? The even is almost come, and here be many bushes and hedges; if he escape and quit himself of this danger, his subtilty is so great that not all the art in the world shall ever again entangle him. If you mean to execute him, then proceed, for before the gallows can be made, it will be dark night.'

At these words *Isegrim*, remembering himself, said, ' There is a pair of gallows near at hand' (and with that fetched a deep sigh), which the cat noting, said, ' Are you afraid, sir *Isegrim*, or is this execution against your mind? You may remember that it was only his work that both your brethren were hanged; and sure had you judgment, you would thank him for the same, and not thus stand trifling time.'

But *Isegrim*, half angry, answered, ' Your anger puts out the eye of your reason, yet had we a halter that would fit his neck, we would soon despatch him.'

Reynard, that had been silent a great while,

said, 'I beseech you, shorten my pain; sir
Tibert hath a cord strong enough, in which
himself was hanged at the priest's house;
besides, he can climb well and swift. O let him
be mine executioner, for it neither becometh
Isegrim nor *Bruin* thus to do to their nephew.
I am sorry I live to see it; but since you are
set to be my hangmen, play your parts and
delay not; go before, *Bruin*, and lead my way;
follow, *Isegrim*, and beware I escape not.'

'You say well,' said *Bruin*, 'and it is the
best counsel I have heard you give.'

So forth they went, and *Isegrim* and all his
friends guarded the fox, leading him by the
neck and other parts of his body. When the
fox felt this usage, he was dismayed, yet said,
'O why do you put yourself, my best kinsman, to this pain, to do me hurt? Believe it, I
could well ask your forgiveness, though my pains
be pleasant unto you, yet well I know, did my
aunt, your wife, understand of my trouble, she
would for old affection's sake not see me thus
tormented. But I am subject to your will, and
can endure your worst malice; as for *Bruin* and
Tibert, I leave my revenge to justice, and wish
you the reward of traitors, if you do not to me
the worst of your powers. I know my worst

fortune, and death can come but once unto me; I wish it were past already, for to me it is no terror; I saw my father die, and how quickly he vanished, therefore the worst of death is familiar unto me.'

Then said *Isegrim*, ' Let us go, for his curse shall not light on me by delaying.'   So he on one side, and *Bruin* on the other, led the poor fox to the gallows ; *Tibert* running before with the halter, hoped to be revenged of his wrong formerly received.   When they were come to the place of execution, the King and Queen, and all the rest of the nobility, took their place to see the fox die.   Then *Reynard*, full of sorrow, and busily bethinking himself how he might escape that danger, and how to enthral and disgrace his proud enemies, and also how to draw the King on his party, said to himself, ' Though the King and many others be offended with me, as they have reason, for I have thoroughly deserved it, nevertheless, yet I hope to live to be their best friend.'

During this meditation the wolf said, ' Sir *Bruin*, now remember your injuries, take your revenge in a full measure, for the day is come we wished for.   *Tibert*, ascend quickly, and bring the rope to the gallows, making a running noose, for this day you shall have your will of your enemy ; and good sir *Bruin*, take heed he escape not, whilst I myself raise up the ladder.'

When all things were prepared, the fox said, 'Now may my heart be heavy, for death stands now in all his horror before me, and I cannot escape ; my dread Lord the King, and you, my Sovereign Lady the Queen, and you, my lords, that stand to behold to see me die, I beseech you grant me this charitable boon, that I may unlock my heart before you, and clear my soul of her burdens, so that hereafter no man may be blamed for me, which done, my death will be easy.'

CHAPTER XII

How Reynard *made his Confession before the King.*

EVERY creature now took compassion on the
fox, and said his request was small, beseeching
the King to grant it, which was done; and
then the fox thus spake: 'Help me, Heaven,
for I see no man here whom I have not
offended; yet was this evil no natural in-
clination in me, for in my youth I was accounted as virtuous as any breathing. This
know, I have played with the lambs all the
day long, and took delight in their pretty
bleating, yet at last in my play I bit one, and
the taste of their blood was so sweet unto me
that I approved the flesh, and both were so
sweet that since I could never forbear it. This
liquorish humour drew me into the woods
amongst the goats, where hearing the bleating
of the little kids, I slew one of them, and after,
two more, which slaughter made me so hardy,

that then I fell to murder hens, geese, and
other poultry. And thus my crimes increased
by custom, and fury so possessed me, that all
was fish which came to my net. After this, in
the winter season, I met with *Isegrim*, where,

as he lay hid under a hollow tree, he unfolded
unto me how he was my uncle, and laid the
pedigree down so plain, that from that day
forth we became fellows and companions; that
knot of friendship I may ever curse, for then
began the flood of our thefts and slaughters.
He stole the great things, I the small; he

murdered nobles, I the mean subjects; and in all our actions his share was still ever the greatest. When he got a ram, a calf, or wether, his fury would hardly afford me the horns to pick on. Nay, when he had an ox, or a cow, after himself, his wife, and his seven children were served, nothing remained to me but the bare bones to pick on. This I speak not in that I wanted (for it is well known I have more plate, jewels, and coin than twenty carts are able to carry), but only to show his ingratitude.'

When the King heard him speak of this infinite treasure and riches, his heart grew inflamed with a desire thereof, and he said, '*Reynard*, where is that treasure you speak of?'

The fox answered, 'My Lord, I shall willingly tell you, for it is true the wealth was stolen, and had it not been stolen in that manner which it was, it had cost your highness your life (which Heaven I beseech keep ever in their protection).'

When the Queen heard that dangerous speech, she started, and said, 'What dangers are these you speak of, *Reynard?* I do command you, upon your soul's health, to unfold these doubtful speeches, and to keep nothing concealed which concerns the life of my dread lord.'

The fox, with a sorrowful and sad countenance, replied to the Queen, 'O my dread Sovereign Lady, at what infinite ease were I, if I might die at this present! But, gracious Madam, your conjuration and the health of mine own soul so prevaileth with me, that I will discharge my conscience, and yet speak nothing but what I will make good with the hazard of my life. It is true, the King should have been pitilessly murdered by his own people, and I must confess by those of my dearest kindred, whom I am unwilling to accuse, did not the health of mine own soul and my fealty to the King command the contrary.'

The King, much perplexed at this discovery, said, ' Is this true, *Reynard*, which you protest ? '

The fox answered, ' Alas, my dread Lord, you see the case wherein I stand, and how small a sand is left in my poor glass to run. Can your Majesty imagine I will now dissemble ? What can the whole world avail me, when my soul perisheth ? '

At that he trembled, and looked so pitifully, that the Queen had great compassion of him, and humbly besought the King, for the safety of his own royal person, to take some pity of the fox, and to command all his subjects to hold their peace, and keep silence till he had spoken the uttermost of his knowledge ; all which was presently done, and the fox proceeded in this manner :

'Since it is the pleasure of my Sovereign Lord the King, and that his royal life lieth in the balance with my present death, I will freely and boldly unfold this capital and foul treason, and in the relation not spare any guilty person for any respect whatsoever, whether it be blood, greatness, or authority.   Know then, my dread Sovereign Lord the King, that my father by a strange accident, digging in the ground, found out King *Ermerick's* treasure, being a mass infinite and innumerable ; of which being possessed, he grew so proud and haughty, that he held in scorn all the beasts of the wilderness, which before had been his kinsmen and companions.   At last he caused *Tibert* the cat to go into the vast forest of *Arden* to *Bruin* the bear, and to tender to him his homage and fealty, saying, " If it would please him to be king, he should come into *Flanders*, where he would show him means

how to set the crown upon his head." *Bruin*
was glad of this embassage (for he was exceeding ambitious, and had long thirsted for
sovereignty), and thereupon came into *Flanders*,
where my father received him nobly.   Then
presently he sent for the wise *Grimbard*, my

nephew, and for *Isegrim* the wolf, and for
Tibert the cat ; then these five coming between
Gaunt and the village called *Elfe*, they held a
solemn council for the space of a whole night, in
which, by the assistance of the evil one, and the
strong confidence of my father's riches, it was
there concluded, that your Majesty should be
forthwith murdered.   And, to effect this, they
took a solemn oath in this manner : the bear,

my father, *Grimbard*, and the cat, laying their hands on *Isegrim's* crown, swore, first to make *Bruin* their king, and to place him in the chair of estate at *Acon*, and to set the imperial diadem on his head; and if by any of your Majesty's blood and alliance they should be gainsaid, that then my father with his treasure should hire those which should utterly chase and root them out of the forest. Now after this determination held and finished, it happened that my nephew *Grimbard*, being on a time high flown with wine, he discovered this dread plot to Dame *Slopecade* his wife, commanded her upon her life to keep secret the same. But she, forgetful of her charge, disclosed it in confession to my wife, as they went a pilgrimage over an heath, with like conjuration of secrecy. But she, woman-like, contained it no longer than till she met with me, and gave me a full knowledge of all that had passed, yet so as by all means I must keep it secret too, for she had sworn by the three kings of *Cologne* never to disclose it. And withal she gave me such assurance by certain tokens, that I right well found all was true which she had spoken; insomuch that the very affright thereof made my hair stand upright,

and my heart became like lead, cold and heavy
in my bosom. This made me call to mind the
story of the frogs, who being free and without
subjection, complained to *Jupiter*, and desired
they might have a king to rule and govern
over them, and he presently sent them a stork,
which ate and devoured them up; so that by
his tyranny they became the most miserable of
all creatures; then they complained again to
Jupiter for redress, but it was then too late, for
they which could not be content with their
freedom must now of necessity suffer in
thraldom.

'Thus I feared it might happen with us,
and thus I sorrowed for your Majesty, although
you little respect my grieving. I know that
ambition of the bear, and his tyranny is so
infinite great, that should the government
come into his hands (as Heaven forbid) the
whole commonwealth will be destroyed. Besides, I know your Majesty of so royal and
princely birth, so mighty, so gracious, and so
merciful, that it had been a horrible exchange
to have seen a ravenous bear sit in the throne
of the royal lion, for there is in the bear and in
his generation more prodigal looseness and in-
constancy than in any beast whatsoever. But

to proceed: from this sorrow I began to meditate how I might undo my father's false and wicked conspiracies, who sought to bring a base traitor and a slave into the throne imperial. For I well perceived as long as he held the treasure, there was a possibility of deposing your Majesty, and this troubled my thought exceedingly, so that I laboured how I might find out where my father's treasure was hid, and to that end I watched and attended night and day in the woods, in the bushes, and in the open fields. Nay, in all places wheresoever my father laid his eyes, there was I ever watching and attending. Now it happened on a time, as I was laid down flat on the ground, I saw my father come running out of a hole, and as soon as he was come out, he gazed round about him, to see if any discovered him. Then seeing the coast clear, he stopped the hole with sand, and made it so even, smooth, and plain, that no curious eye could discern a difference betwixt it and the other earth. And where the print of his foot remained, that with his tail he stroked over, and with his mouth so smoothed, that no man might perceive it; and indeed that and many other subtilties I learned of him there at that instant. When he had

thus finished, away he went towards the village about his private affairs; then went I presently towards the hole, and notwithstanding all his subtilty I quickly found it out, then entered I the cave, where I found that innumerable quantity of treasure which cannot be expressed. I took *Ermelin* my wife to help me, and we

ceased not, day nor night, with infinite great toil and labour, to carry and convey away this treasure to another place much more convenient for us, where we laid it safe from the search of any creature.   Now during the time that my wife and I were thus employed, my father was in consultation with the rest of the traitors, about the death of the King; in which consultation it was concluded that *Isegrim* the wolf should travel over all the kingdom, and promise to all beasts that would take wages, and acknowledge *Bruin* for their sovereign, and defend his title, a full year's pay before-hand. And in this journey my father accompanied him, carrying letters patent signed to that purpose, little suspecting that he was robbed of the wealth which should supply his

treason. When this negotiation was finished between *Elve* and *Soame*, and a world of valiant soldiers raised against the beginning of the next spring, then they returned to *Bruin* and his consorts, to whom they declared the many perils they had escaped in the dukedom of *Saxony*, where they were pursued by huntsmen and hounds, so as they hardly escaped with life. After this relation they showed *Bruin* their muster rolls, which pleased him exceeding much, for there was of *Isegrim's* lineage about twelve hundred sworn to the action, besides the bear's own kindred, the fox's, the cat's, and the dassen's, all which would be in readiness upon an hour's warning. All this I found out, I praise Heaven, by perfect intelligence ; now things being brought to this perfection, my father went to his cave of treasure, but when he found it open, spoiled, and ransacked, it is not in me to express the infinite agony and sorrow he fell into, that grief converting to madness, and madness to desperation, suddenly he went to the next tree and hanged himself.

'Thus by my art only was the treason of *Bruin* defeated, for which I now suffer ; from hence sprang all misfortune, as thus : these foul traitors, *Bruin* and *Isegrim*, being of the King's privatest council, and sitting in high and great authority, tread upon me, poor *Reynard*, and work my disgrace ; notwithstanding, for your Majesty's sake, I have lost my natural father. O my dread Lord, what is he, or who can tender you a better affection, thus to lose himself to save you ?'

The King and Queen having great hope

to get this inestimable treasure from *Reynard*, took him from the gibbet, and entreated him to unfold where this great treasure was.

But the fox replied, 'O my Lord, shall I make mine enemies my heirs? shall these traitors which take away my life, and would devour yours, be possessed of the good I enjoy? No, that is a madness I will never die guilty of.'

Then said the Queen, 'Fear not, *Reynard*, the King shall save your life, and grant you pardon, and you shall henceforth swear faith and true allegiance to his Majesty.'

The fox answered, 'Dearest Madam, if the King out of his royal nature will give credit to my truth, and forgive my former offences, there was never King so rich as I will make him.'

Then the King staying the Queen, said, 'Madam, will you believe the fox? know you not that it is his natural quality to lie, steal, and deceive?'

The Queen answered, 'My dear Lord, now you may boldly believe him, for howsoever in his prosperity he was full of errors, yet now you may see he is changed. Why, he spareth not to accuse his own father, nay,

Grimbard, his dearest nephew and kinsman; had he dissembled, he might have laid his imputations on other beasts, and not on those he loveth most entirely.'

'Well, Madam,' said the King, 'you shall at this time rule me, and all the offences of the fox I will clearly pardon; yet with this protestation, that if ever again he offend in the smallest crime whatsoever, that not only himself, but his whole generation I will utterly root out of my dominions.'

The fox looked sadly when the King spake thus, but was inwardly most infinitely glad at his heart, and said, 'My dread Lord, it were a huge shame in me, should I speak any untruths in this great presence.'

Then the King taking a straw from the ground, pardoned the fox of all his trespasses which either he or his father had ever committed. If the fox now began to smile, it was no wonder, the sweetness of life required it; yet he fell down before the King and Queen, and humbly thanked them for mercy, protesting that for that favour he would make them the richest princes in the world. And at these words the fox took up a straw, and proffered it unto the King, and said to him, ' My dread Lord, I beseech your Majesty to receive this pledge as a surrender unto your Majesty of all the treasure that the great King *Ermerick* was master of, with

which I freely infeoff you, out of my mere voluntary and free motion.'

At these words the King received the straw, and smiling, gave the fox great thanks for the same. But the fox laughed outright to think of the abuse; from that day forward

no man's counsel prevailed with the King as
the fox's, which the fox seeing, said to the
King, 'My gracious Lord, you shall understand that at the west side of *Flanders*, there
standeth a wood called *Hustreloe*, near which
runneth a river named *Crekenpit;* this is a
wilderness so vast and impassable, that hardly
in all the year there cometh either man or
woman in the same. In it I have hid this
treasure, whither I would have your Majesty
and the Queen to go, for I know none but
yourselves whom I dare trust in so great
design ; and when your highness comes thither,
you shall find two birchen trees growing by
the pit, into which you shall enter, and there
you shall find the treasure, which consisteth
of coin, rich jewels, and the wealthy crown
which King *Ermerick* wore. With this crown
Bruin the bear should have been crowned, if
his treason had succeeded according to his
determination. There shall you see also many
rich and costly precious stones, of which, when
you are possessed, then remember the love
of your servant *Reynard.*'

The King answered, 'Sir *Reynard*, you
must yourself help me to dig for this treasure,
for else I shall never find it. I have heard

named *Paris*, *London*, *Aix*, and *Cologne*, but *Crekenpit* I never heard of, therefore, I fear, you dissemble.'

The fox blushed at those words, yet with a bold countenance he said, 'Is your Majesty so doubtful of my faith? nay, then I will approve my words by public testimony'; and with that he called forth *Kyward* the hare from among the rest of the beasts, and commanded him to come before the King, charging him upon his faith and allegiance which he bore to the King and Queen, to answer truly to such questions as he should ask him.

The hare answered, 'I will speak truth in all things, though I were sure to die for the same.'

Then the fox said, 'Know you not where *Crekenpit* standeth?'

'Yes,' said the hare, 'I have known it any time these dozen years; it standeth in a wood called *Hustreloe*, upon a vast and wide wilderness, where I have endured much torment both of hunger and cold. Besides, it was there where father *Simony* the friar made false coin, with which he supported himself and his fellows. Yet that was before I and *Ring* the hound became companions.'

'Well,' said the fox, 'you have spoken sufficiently, go to your place again'; so away went the hare. Then said the fox, 'My Sovereign Lord the King, what say you now to my relation—am I worthy your belief or no?'

The King said, 'Yes, *Reynard*, and I beseech thee excuse my jealousies, it was my ignorance which did thee evil; therefore forthwith make preparation that we may go to this pit where the treasure lieth.'

The fox answered, 'Alas, my Lord, do you imagine that I would not fain go with you? if it were so that I might go without your dishonour, which I cannot do; for you shall understand (though it be my disgrace) that when *Isegrim* the wolf, in the evil one's name, would needs grow religious and turn a monk, that then the permission of meat which was for six monks, was too little for him alone. Whereupon he complained so pitifully unto me, that I, commiserating his case, being my kinsman, gave him counsel to run away, which he did. Whereupon I stand accursed, and excommunicated under the Pope's sentence, and am determined to-morrow, as soon as the sun riseth, to take my way towards *Rome* to be absolved, and from *Rome* I intend to cross the seas to the Holy Land, and will never return again to my native country, till I have done so much good, and satisfied for my sins, that I may with honour and reputation attend on your highness's person.'

The King, hearing this, said, 'Since you stand accursed in the censures of the Church, I may not have you about me, and therefore I will at this time take *Kyward* the hare, and some other with me to *Crekenpit*, and only command you, *Reynard*, as you respect my favour, to clear yourself of his holiness's curse.'

'My Lord,' said the fox, 'it is the only reason of my going to *Rome*; neither will I rest night nor day till I have gotten a full absolution.'

'The course you take is good,' said the King, 'go on and prosper in your intent and purpose.'

CHAPTER XIII

How Reynard *the Fox was honoured of all beasts by the King's commandment.*

As soon as this conference was ended, the royal King mounted upon a high throne made in manner of a scaffold, made of fair squared stone, and then commanded a general silence amongst all his subjects, and that every one should take his place according to his birth, or dignity in office, only the fox was placed between the King and the Queen.

Then said the King, 'Hear, all you noblemen, knights, gentlemen, and others of inferior quality; this *Reynard*, one of the chief and supreme officers of my household, whose offences had brought him to the least reckoning of his life, as being in the hands of the law and justice, hath this day, in requital of these injuries, done that noble and worthy service to the State that both myself and my Queen stand bound to render him our best grace and favour. Therefore know, that for divers things best known unto ourselves, we have freely given pardon to all his offences, and restored back to

him whatsoever to us was confiscate; therefore, henceforth I command all of you, upon the pain and hazard of your dearest lives, that you fail not from this day forward to do all reverence and honour not only to *Reynard* himself, but also to his wife and children; whensoever or

wheresoever you shall meet them, whether by
night or by day. And let not any one hereafter
be so audacious as to trouble mine ears with any
more complaints of him; for his wickedness
he hath cast behind him, and will no more be
guilty of wrongdoing, which to effect the better,
to-morrow very early he taketh his journey
towards *Rome*, where from the Pope he will
purchase a free pardon and indulgence for all
his offences, and then will go on pilgrimage to
the Holy Land.'

This speech, when *Tisellin* the raven heard,
he flew to *Bruin*, *Isegrim*, and *Tibert*, and
said, 'Wretched creatures, how are your
fortunes changed! or how can you endure to
hear these tidings? Why, *Reynard* is now a
courtier, a counsellor, nay, the prime favourite;
his offences are forgiven, and you are all
betrayed, and sold unto bondage.'

Isegrim answered, 'It is impossible, *Tisellin*,
nor can such a thing be suffered.'

'Do not deceive yourselves,' said the raven,
'for it is as true as that now I speak it.'

Then went the wolf and the bear to the
King, but the cat stayed, and was so sore
affrighted with the news, that to purchase the
fox's friendship again, he would not only have

forgiven the evils received, but willingly have run into a second hazard. But now *Isegrim*, with great majesty and pride tracing over the fields, came before the King and Queen, and with most bitter and cruel words inveighed against the fox in such a passionate and impudent manner, that the King, being infinitely moved with displeasure, caused the wolf and the bear to be presently arrested upon high treason; which suddenly was done with all violence and fury, and they were bound hand and foot so fast, that they could neither stir nor move from the place where they were couched.

Now when the fox had thus enthralled and entangled them, he so laboured with the Queen, that he got leave to have so much of the bear's skin as would make him a large scrip for his journey; which granted, he wanted nothing but a strong pair of shoes to defend his feet from the stones in his travel; whereupon he said to the Queen, 'Madam, I am your pilgrim, and if it would please your Majesty but to take it into your consideration, you shall find that sir *Isegrim* hath a pair of shoon, excellent long-lasting ones, which would you vouchsafe to bestow upon me, I should pray for your Majesty's soul in all my travel, above any charitable devotion. Also mine aunt, Dame *Ereswine*, hath other two shoes, which would your Majesty bestow upon me, I should be most infinitely bound to you, nor should you do to her any wrong, because she goes seldom abroad.'

The Queen replied, ' *Reynard*, I can perceive how you can want such shoes, for your journey is full of labour and difficulty, both in respect of the stony mountains and the gravelly ways, and therefore you shall have (though it touch their life never so nearly) from each of them a pair of shoes to accomplish and finish your journey.'

CHAPTER XIV

How Isegrim *and his wife* Ereswine *had their shoes plucked off, for* Reynard *to wear to* Rome.

AFTER the fox had made this petition, *Isegrim* was taken, and his shoes pulled off in most cruel and violent manner, so that all the veins and sinews lay naked, nor durst the poor massacred wolf either complain or resist. After he had been thus tormented, then Dame *Ereswine* his wife was used on the same manner on her hinder feet, as her husband was on his forefeet; which the fox seeing, said to her in a scornful manner, 'Dear aunt, how much am I bound to you that take all this pains for my sake! Questionless, you shall be a sharer in my pilgrimage, and take part in the pardon I shall bring from beyond the seas by the help of your shoes.'

Then *Ereswine* (though speech were troublesome to her) said, 'Well, sir *Reynard*, you have your will accomplished, yet Heaven, I hope, will requite the misdoer.'

This she said, but her husband and the bear lay mute, for their wounds were grievous unto

them; and surely had the cat been there also, he had not escaped some extreme punishment. The next morning, very early, *Reynard*, causing his shoes to be well oiled, put them on, and made them as fit to his feet as they were to the wolves', and then went to the King and Queen, and said, 'My dread Lord and Lady, your poor subject voweth before your Majesties, humbly beseeching your highnesses to vouchsafe to deliver me my mail and my staff blessed, according to the custom due unto pilgrims.'

This said, the King sent for *Bellin* the ram, and commanded him to say solemn mass before the fox, and to deliver him his staff and his mail; but the ram refused, saying, 'My Lord, I dare not, for he hath confessed he is in the Pope's curse.'

And the King said, 'What of that? Have not our doctors told us, that if a man commit all the sins in the world, yet if he repent himself, be shriven, do penance, and walk as the priest shall instruct him, that all is clearly forgiven him? and hath not *Reynard* done all this?'

Then answered *Bellin*, 'Sir, I am loath to meddle herein, yet if your Majesty will bear me harmless against the bishop of *Prendesor*, my ordinary, and against the archdeacon *Loosuynd*, and *Rapiamus* his official, I will effect your commandment.'

At this the King grew angry, and said, 'I scorn to be beholden unto you'; but when the ram saw the King offended, he shook for fear, and ran presently to the altar, and sang mass, and used many ceremonies over the fox, who gave little respect unto them, more than the desire he had to enjoy the honour.

Now when *Bellin* the ram had finished his orisons, he presently hung about *Reynard's* neck his mail, which was made of the bear's skin, and put into his right foot a palmer's staff; and thus being furnished of all things, he looked sadly upon the King, as if he had been loath to depart, and feigned to weep (though sorrow and he were never farther asunder), only his worst grief was, that all in that presence were not in the same case that the bear and the wolf were. Yet he took his leave of them, and desired every one to pray for him, as he would pray for them; and then offering to depart (for knowing his own knavery, he was very desirous to be gone).

The King said, 'Sir *Reynard*, I am sorry we must part thus suddenly.'

Then said the fox, ' There is no remedy, my Lord, nor ought I to be slow in so devout an action.'

Then the King took leave, and commanded all that were about him, but the bear and the wolf, to attend *Reynard* some part of his journey. O he that had seen how gallant and personable *Reynard* was, and how well his staff and his mail became him, as also how fit his shoes were for his feet, it could not have chosen but have stirred in him very much laughter. Yet the fox carried himself outwardly very demurely, however inwardly he smiled at the abuses he had cast amongst them, especially to see his enemies now his attendants, and the King, whom he had most palpably wronged with false lies, aiding to all his vain desires, and accompanying him also as if he had been his companion.

But the fox being now started on his way, he said to the King, ' I beseech your Majesty trouble yourself no further, but in respect of your ease, and the danger might happen to your royal person, for you have arrested two capital traitors, who, if in your absence they should get at liberty, the danger were infinite which might ensue thereon.'

And this said, he stood upon his hinder feet, and entreated the beasts that were in his company, and would be partakers of his pardon, that they would pray for him; which done, he departed from the King with an exceeding sad and heavy countenance. Then turning to *Kyward* the hare, and *Bellin* the ram, he said with a smiling countenance, ' My best friends, ·

shall we part thus soon? I know your loves will not leave me yet; with you two I was never offended, and your conversations are agreeable to my nature. For you are mild, loving, and courteous; religious, and full of wise counsel, even such as myself was when I was first a recluse; if you have a few green leaves, or a little grass, you are well content as with all the bread and flesh in the world, and you are temperate and modest.'

And thus with a world of such like flattering words he enticed these two, that they were content to go along with him.

CHAPTER XV

How Kyward *the Hare was slain by* Reynard *the* *Fox, and sent by the Ram to the King.*

THUS marched these three together, and when *Reynard* was come to the gates of his own house he said to *Bellin*, 'Cousin, I will entreat you to stay here without a little, whilst I and *Kyward* go in, for I would have him a witness to some private passages betwixt me and my wife.'

Bellin was well content, and so the fox and the hare went into *Malepardus*, where they found Dame *Ermelin* lying on the ground with her younglings about her, who had sorrowed exceedingly for the loss and danger of her husband; but when she saw his return, her joy was ten times doubled. But beholding his mail, his staff, and his shoes, she grew into great admiration, and said, ' Dear husband, how have you fared?' to whom he delivered from point to point all that had passed with him at the King's court, as well his danger as release, and that now he was to go a pilgrimage, having left *Bruin* and *Isegrim* two pledges for him till his return.

As for *Kyward*, he said the King had bestowed him upon them, to do with him what

they pleased, affirming that *Kyward* was the first that had complained of him, for which, questionless, he vowed to be sharply revenged.

When *Kyward* heard these words he was much appalled, and would fain have fled away, but he could not; for the fox had got between him and the gate, who presently seized the

hare by the neck, at which the hare cried unto
Bellin for help, but could not be heard, for the
fox in a trice had torn out his throat; which
done, he, his wife, and young ones feasted
therewith merrily, eating the flesh, and drinking the blood to the King's health; but
Ermelin, growing suspicious, said, 'I fear,
Reynard, you mock me; as you love me, tell
me how you sped at the court.'

Then he told her how extremely he had
flattered the King and the Queen, and abused
them with a feigned promise of treasure that
was not, insomuch, that he knew when it
should come to be revealed, the King would
seek all the means he could to destroy him.

'Therefore, wife,' said he, 'there is no
remedy but we must steal from hence into
some other forest where we may live in better
safety, and in a place more fruitful, where we
shall have all the delicate meats that can be
wished for; clear springs, fresh rivers, cool
shades, and wholesome air. Here I know is
no abiding, and now I have gotten my thumb
out of the King's mouth, I will no more come
within the danger of his talons.'

'Yet,' said *Ermelin*, 'I have no fancy to
go from hence to a place where I am utterly

unacquainted; here we possess all that we desire, and you are a lord over all that lives about you, and it is but an indiscreet hazard to change a certain good for a hoped contentment; besides, we are here safe enough, and should the King besiege us never so straitly, yet have we so many passages and by-holes, that he can cut from us neither relief nor liberty. O what reason have we then to fly beyond seas? but you have sworn it, that's my vexation.'

'Nay, Dame,' said the fox, 'grieve not at that; the more forsworn, the less forlorn; besides, I have heard some say, that a forced oath is no oath, nor do I make account that this pilgrimage will avail me a rush; and therefore I am resolved, and will not start from hence, but follow thy counsel. If the King do hunt after me, I will guard myself as well as I am able, and against his power apply my policy; so that being forced to open my sack, let him not blame me if he catch hurt by his own fury.'

All this while stood *Bellin* the ram at the gate, and grew exceeding angry both against the fox and the hare, that they made him wait so long; and therefore called out aloud for *Reynard* to come away, which, when *Reynard* heard, he went forth, and said softly to the ram,

'Good *Bellin*, be not offended, for *Kyward* is in earnest conference with his dearest aunt, and entreated me to say unto you, that if you would please to walk before, he would speedily overtake you, for he is light of foot, and speedier than you; nor will his aunt part with him thus suddenly, for she and her children are much perplexed at my departure.'

'Ay, but,' quoth *Bellin*, 'methought I heard *Kyward* cry for help.'

'How, cry for help? Can you imagine he shall receive hurt in my house? Far be such a thought from you; but I will tell you the reason. As soon as we were come into my house, and that *Ermelin* my wife understood of my pilgrimage, presently she fell down in a swoon, which, when *Kyward* saw, he cried aloud, " O *Bellin*, come, help my aunt, she dies, she dies ! " '

Then said the ram, 'In sadness I mistook the cry, and thought the hare had been in danger.'

'It was your too much care of him,' said the fox, 'but before he should have any injury in my house, I would leave to respect either wife or children. But letting this discourse pass, you remember, *Bellin*, that yesterday the King and his council commanded me, that before I departed from the land, I should send unto him two letters, which I have made ready, and will entreat you, my dearest cousin, to bear them to his Majesty.'

The ram answered, ' I would willingly do you the service if there be nothing but honourable matter contained in your letters; but I am unprovided of anything to carry them in.'

The fox said, ' That is provided for you already, for you shall have my mail which you may conveniently hang about your neck; I know they will be thankfully received of his Majesty, for they contain matter of great importance.'

Then *Bellin* promised to carry them ; so the fox returned into his house, and took the mail, and put therein the head of *Kyward*, and brought it to the ram, and gave him a great charge not to look therein, till it was presented to the King, as he did expect the King's favour; and that he might further endear himself with his Majesty, he bade the ram take upon him the inditing of the letters, ' which will be so pleasing to the King, that questionless he will pour upon you many favours.'

The ram was exceeding glad of this advice, and thanked the fox, saying, ' That the favours

he did him should not die unrequited ; and I
know it will be much to mine honour when the
King shall think I am able to indite with so
great perfection ; for I know there be many in
these days as ignorant as myself that are risen
to high promotion, only by taking upon them
the worth of other men's labours ; and therefore,

why may not I run the same course also? Yet
I pray you, *Reynard*, further advise me : is it
meet that I take *Kyward* the hare along with
me ? '

'O by no means,' said the fox ; 'let him come
after you, for I know his aunt will not yet part
with him. Besides, I have other secret things
to impart to him, which may not yet be revealed.'

This said, *Bellin* took leave of the fox and went toward the court, in which journey he made such speed that he came thither before noon, where he found the King in his palace sitting amongst the nobility.

The King wondered when he saw the ram come in with the mail which was made of the

bear's skin, and said, 'Whence comest thou, *Bellin*, and where is the fox, that you have that mail about you?'

Bellin answered, 'My dread Lord, I attended the noble fox to his house, where, after some repose, he desired me to bear certain letters to your Majesty of infinite great importance, to which I easily consented. Whereupon he delivered me the letters enclosed in this mail, which letters myself had formerly indited, and I doubt not but are such as will give your highness both contentment and satisfaction.'

Presently he commanded the letters to be delivered to *Bocart*, his secretary, who was an excellent linguist, and understood all languages, that he might read them publicly; so he and *Tibert* the cat took the mail from *Bellin's* neck, and opening the same, instead of letters they drew out the head of *Kyward* the hare, at which, being amazed, they said, 'Woe, and alas, what letters call you these? Believe it, my dread Lord, here is nothing but the head of poor murdered *Kyward*.'

Which the King seeing, he said, 'Alas, how unfortunate was I to believe the traitorous fox?'

And with that, being oppressed with anger, grief, and shame, he held down his head for a good space, and so did the Queen also; but in the end, shaking his curled locks, he groaned out such a dreadful noise, that all the beasts of the forest did tremble to hear it.

Then spake sir *Firapell* the leopard, who was the King's nearest kinsman, and said,

'Why is your Majesty thus vexed in heart? This sorrow might serve for the Queen's funeral. I do beseech you, assuage your anguish; are not you King and master of this country, and are not all things subject to your power?'

The King replied, 'Cousin, this is a mischief beyond endurance; I am betrayed by a base villain, and a traitor, and have been made to wrong and abuse my best friends and subjects, even those of my blood, and nearest counsel. I mean the stout *Bruin*, and valiant *Isegrim*, whose wrongs speak loud to my dishonour, yet in myself I found an unwillingness thereto, only my Queen's pity working upon the easiness of my belief, hath made me guilty of that which will evermore grieve me.'

'Why,' said the leopard, 'what of all this? You are above your injuries, and with one smile can salve the greatest wound that can be made in honour; you have power to recompense, and what reputation is it that reward will not sawder? As for the bear which lost his skin, the wolf, and his wife, Dame *Ereswine*, that lost their shoes, you may in recompense (since *Bellin* hath confessed himself a party in this foul murder) bestow

him and his substance on the parties grieved;
as for *Reynard*, we will go and besiege his
castle, and having arrested his person, hang
him up by the law of arms without further
trial.'

CHAPTER XVI

How Bellin *the Ram and his lineage were given to the Bear and the Wolf.*

To this motion of the leopard the King consented, so that *Firapell* forthwith went to the prison, where the bear and the wolf were, and said, ' My lords, I bring a free and general pardon from the King, with his love and a recognition of your injuries, which to recompense in some large manner out of his princely bounty, he is pleased to bestow upon you both *Bellin* the ram and his whole generation, with whatsoever they possess, and is now confiscate to his Majesty, to hold from henceforth to you and yours till doomsday; with full commission to slay, kill, and devour them wheresoever you find them, be it in woods, fields, or mountains. And also the King granted unto you full power to hunt, kill, or wound *Reynard* the fox wheresoever you

find him or any of his lineage or generation;
and of this great privilege you shall receive

letters patent at your pleasure, with only a
reservation of your fealty and homage to be due
to his Majesty, which I advise you to accept,
for it will redound much to your honours.'

Thus was the peace made between the King and these nobles by the leopard, and *Bellin* the ram was forthwith slain by them; and all these privileges doth the wolf hold to this hour, nor could ever any reconcilement be made between them and the ram's kindred. When this peace was thus finished, the King, for joy thereof, proclaimed a feast to be held for twelve days after, which was done with all solemnity.

To this feast came all manner of wild beasts, for it was universally known through the whole kingdom, nor was there wanting any delight or pleasure that could be imagined, as music, dancing, masking, and all princely re-creations; as for several meats, they were in that abundance, that the court seemed a store-house which could not be emptied. Also to this feast resorted abundance of feathered fowl, and all other creatures that held peace with his Majesty, and no one missing but the fox only.

Now after this feast had thus continued in all pomp the space of eight days, about high noon came *Laprell* the coney before the King and Queen, as they sat at dinner, and with a heavy and lamentable voice said, 'My gracious and great Lord, have pity upon my misery, and attend my complaint, which is of great violence, force, and murder, which *Reynard* the fox would yesterday have committed against me.   As I passed by the castle of *Malepardus*, where, standing without his gates, attired like a pilgrim, I supposing to pass peaceably by him towards my nest, he crossed my way,

saying his beads so devoutly, that I saluted him ; but he, returning no answer, stretched forth his right foot and gave me such a blow on the neck between the head and shoulders, that I imagined my head had been stricken from my body ; but yet so much memory was left me that I leaped from his claws, though most grievously hurt and wounded.   At this he grieved extremely, because I escaped; only of one of my ears he utterly deprived me, which I beseech your Majesty in your royal nature to pity, and that this bloody murderer may not live thus to afflict your poor subjects.'

Now whilst the coney was thus speaking to the King, there came flying into the court *Corbaut* the rook, who, coming before the

King, said, 'Great King, I beseech you, vouchsafe to hear me, and pity the complaint I shall utter. So it is, that I went this morning with *Sharpbeak* my wife to recreate ourselves on the heath, and there we found *Reynard* the fox laid on the ground like a dead carcass, his eyes staring, his tongue lolling out of his mouth, like a dead hound, so that we, wondering at his strange plight, began to feel and touch his

body, but found no life therein at all. Then
went my wife (poor careful soul), laid her head
to his mouth, to see if he drew any breath,
which she had no sooner done, but the foul
murderer, awaiting his time, snatched her head
into his mouth, and bit it quite off. At that I
shrieked out and cried, "Woe is me, what
misfortunes are these?"

'But presently the murderer started up,
and reached at me with such a bloody intent,
that with much trembling and anguish I was
fain to fly up to a tree, where I saw him
devour up my wife in such terrible manner,
that the very thought is death to me in the
repeating.

'This massacre finished, the murderer departed, and I went to the place and gathered
the feathers of my lost wife, which here I
humbly present before your Majesty, beseeching you to do me justice, and in such
manner to revenge mine injury, that the world
may speak fame of your great excellence.
For thus to suffer your laws, protections, and
safe-conducts to be violated and broken, will
be such disreputation and scandal to your
crown and dignity, that your very neighbours
and colleagues will note and point at your

remissness ; besides, the sufferance of the evil
will make you guilty of the trespasses which
arise from such sufferance.   But to your
great considerations I leave it, since I know
your Majesty's own goodness will make you
careful of your honour and royalty.'

CHAPTER XVII

How the King was angry at these complaints, took counsel for revenge, and how Reynard *was fore-warned by* Grimbard *the Brock.*

THE royal King was much moved with anger when he heard these complaints both of the coney and the rook, so that his eyes darted out fire amongst the beams of majesty; his countenance was dreadful and cruel to look on, and the whole court trembled to behold him. In the end he said, 'By my crown and the truth I evermore reverence and owe unto the Queen my wife, I will so revenge these outrages committed against my crown and dignity, that goodness shall adore me, and the wicked shall die with the remembrance; his falsehood and flattery shall no more get belief in me. Is this his journey to *Rome* and to the *Holy Land?* Are these the fruits of his mail, his staff, and other ornaments becoming a devout pilgrim? Well, he shall find the reward of his treasons; but it was not my belief, but the persuasion of my Queen; nor am I the first that hath been deceived by that soft gender, since many great spirits have fallen through their enticements.'

This said, he commanded all that were about him, all noble, worthy, and very discreet spirits, to assist him with their counsel, and to lay him down such sure ground for his revenge, that his honour and royalty might be anew revived, and every offender made to know and feel the heavy price for their most unjust actions.

Isegrim the wolf and *Bruin* the bear, hearing the King's words, were wonderfully well repaid, and doubted not but now to gain their full revenge against *Reynard;* yet still they kept silence and spake not a word. Insomuch that the King being much moved with their dumbness, and noting that none durst freely deliver their opinions, he began to bend his forehead.

But the Queen, after solemn reverence, said to the King, '*Mon Sire, pour Dieu croyez mie toutes choses qu'on vous dira, et ne jurez point légèrement*, Sir, it is not the part of any excellent wisdom to believe or protest in anything till the matter be made most apparent

and pregnant to his knowledge. Neither
should both his ears be engaged to any complaint, but one ever reserved to entertain the
defence of any accused; for many times the
accuser exceedeth the accused in injury, and
therefore *Audire alteram partem*, to hear the
other party, is the act of perfect justice. For
my own part, howsoever I have erred, yet I
have strong ground for my persuasion, and
whether *Reynard* be good or bad, yet it stands
with your Excellency not to proceed against
him but by the true form of your laws; for he
hath no power to escape you, but must obey
whatsoever your severity can impose upon
him.'

When the Queen had thus spoken, *Firapell*
the leopard, to second her entreaty, said, ' My
Lord, the Queen hath spoken graciously, and I
see not wherein your Majesty can stray from
her judgment; therefore let him take the due
trial of your laws, and being found guilty of the
trespasses whereof he is accused, let him be
summoned, and if he appear not before your
feast be ended, to clear himself, or submit to
your mercy, then may your Highness proceed
against him as it shall seem best to your
pleasure.'

To this speech *Isegrim* the wolf replied, 'Sir *Firapell*, for my own part, I think not any in this assembly will dissent from your counsel, so it may stand with the pleasure of my Lord the King. Yet this I dare maintain, that however *Reynard* shall clear himself of these and a thousand such like trespasses which shall be brought against him, yet I have that lodged in my bosom which shall approve he hath forfeited his life; but at this time his absence shall make me silent, only touching the treasure of which he hath informed his Majesty to lie at *Crekenpit* in *Hustreloe*, there never came a falser information from the mouth of any creature; for it was a lie made out of malice to wrong me and the bear, and get himself liberty to rob and spoil all that pass by his house as now he doth; but, notwithstanding, I hold it meet that all things be done as shall seem good to his Majesty, or you, sir *Firapell*. Yet this believe, that if he had meant to have appeared, he had been here long since, for he hath had summons given him by the King's messenger.'

To this the King answered, 'I will have no other course of summoning him, but command all that owe me allegiance, or respect mine honour, that forthwith they make themselves ready for the war; and at the end of six days appear before me with their bows, guns, bumbards, pikes, and halberds; some on horseback, some on foot, for I will besiege *Malepardus* instantly, and destroy *Reynard* and his generation from the earth for ever; this if any dislike, let him turn his back, that I may know him for mine enemy.'

And they all cried with one voice, 'We are ready to attend your Majesty.'

When *Grimbard* the brock heard this determination he grew exceeding sorry, though his sorrow was desperate, and stealing from the rest of the company, he ran with all speed possible to *Malepardus*, neither sparing bush nor brier, pale nor rail; and as he went he said to himself, 'Alas, my dear uncle *Reynard*, into what hazards art thou drawn, having but one step betwixt thee and thy death, or at the best thine everlasting banishment? Well may I grieve for thee, since thou art the top and honour of my house, art wise and politic, and a friend to thy friends, when they stand in need of thy counsel, for with thy sweet language thou canst enchant all creatures; but all is now bootless.'

With such manner of lamentations as these, came *Grimbard* unto *Malepardus*, and found his uncle *Reynard* standing at the castle gates, who had newly gotten two young pigeons as they came creeping out of their nest to try how they could learn to fly. But now beholding his nephew *Grimbard*, he stayed, and said, 'Welcome, my best beloved nephew, the only one I esteem above all my kindred; surely you have run exceeding fast, for you are wonderfully hot; what news, man, how run the squares at the court?'

'Oh,' said *Grimbard*, 'exceeding ill with you, for you have forfeited both your life, honour, and estate. The King is up in arms against you with horsemen, footmen, and soldiers innumerable; besides, *Isegrim* and *Bruin* are now in more favour with his Majesty than I am with you, therefore it is high time you have great care of yourself, for their envy hath touched you to the quick; they have informed against you, that you are a thief and a murderer; and to second their informations, *Laprell* the coney and *Corbaut* the rook have made heinous complaints against you, so that but your shameful death, I see no escape or freedom.'

'Tush,' said the fox, 'my dear nephew, if this be the worst, let no sorrow affright you; but let us be cheerful and pleasant together, for though the King and all the court would swear my death, yet will I be exalted above them all. Well may they prate and jangle, and tire themselves with their counsels; but without the help of my wit and policy, neither can the court nor commonwealth have any long continuance. Come, then, my best nephew, let us enter into my castle and feast; I have here a pair of fat pigeons for you, which are meat of pure and light digestion; I love not anything better; they are young and tender, and may be almost swallowed whole, for their bones are little other than blood. Yet come, I say, my wife *Ermelin* will receive you kindly; but by all means report not to her of any dangers, for she is of soft and melting temper, and it might strike her into sudden sickness, for women are apt to entertain grief. When we have feasted, I will then to-morrow early in the morning go with you to the court, and if I can but obtain speech with the King, I shall gall some deep enough; only this I desire, dear nephew, at your hands, that you will stand to me, as one friend and kinsman ought to do to another.'

'Doubt me not,' said *Grimbard*, 'for both my life and goods shall be at your service.'

'I thank you, nephew,' said the fox, 'and you shall not find me ungrateful.'

'Sir,' said the brock, 'be bold of this, that you shall come and make your answer before the lords freely, for none shall dare to arrest or hold you, for that favour the Queen and the leopard have purchased from the King.'

'I am glad of that,' said the fox, 'nor care I then a hair for their worst malice.'

And this said, they went into *Malepardus*, and found *Ermelin* sitting among her younglings, who presently arose, and received the brock with all reverence, and he on the other part saluted her and her children with all courtesy. Presently the two pigeons were made ready, and they supped together, each taking their part, though none had so much as they desired.

Then said the fox, 'Nephew, how like you my children *Rossel* and *Reynardine*? I hope they will do honour to our family; they are towardly, I assure you, for the one lately caught

a chicken, and the other hath killed a pullet; they are also good duckers, and can both deceive the lapwing and the mallard. I tell you true, I dare already adventure them far, only I mean first to instruct them how to escape the gins, and to avoid both the hunts-man and his hounds. They are of the right

hair, nephew, and like me both in countenance
and quality; they play grinning, entrap sooth-
ing, and kill smiling; this is the true nature of
the fox, and in this they are perfect, which is
great pride unto me.'

CHAPTER XVIII

How the Fox, *repenting his sins, doth make his confession and is absolved by the* Brock.

' UNCLE,' said the brock, 'you may be proud that you have such toward children, and I rejoice because they are of my blood.'

' I thank you, nephew,' said the fox, ' but I know your journey hath made you weary, therefore you shall go to your rest'; to which the brock consented, so they laid them down upon straw litter, and all slept soundly but the fox, whose heart was heavy with sorrow, and he lay studying how he might best excuse himself before the King.

But as soon as the morning began to rise from the tops of the mountains, he arose and went with *Grimbard* towards the court; yet before he went, he took leave of his wife and children, and said, ' Think not mine absence long, dear wife and children, for I must go to the court with my cousin *Grimbard*, and though my stay be more than ordinary, yet take no affright thereat, and what tidings soever you hear, yet consider all things for the best, and be careful of yourselves, and keep my castle close and well guarded; as for myself, doubt not but I will defeat all mine enemies.'

'Alas, *Reynard*,' said his wife, 'what moves you to take this sudden journey? The last time you were at the court you know what dangers you escaped, and you vowed never to see it again. Will you now run a second hazard?'

'Dame,' said the fox, 'the occurrences of the world are divers and uncertain, and we are subject to the strokes of fortune; but rest you content, there is necessity that I go, and I hope my stay shall not be above five days at the uttermost'; and so embracing his wife and children, he took leave and departed.

And as they journeyed over the heath, *Reynard* said to the brock, 'Nephew, since I was last shriven I have committed many sins, therefore, I beseech you, let me make before you my confession, that I may pass with less trouble through my worst dangers.'

Then he proceeded and said, 'It is true, nephew, that I made the bear receive a great wound for the mail which I did cut off his skin; and I caused the wolf and his wife to be stripped of their shoes; I appeased the King only with falsehood. I feigned a conspiracy against his Majesty's life by the bear and the wolf, when there was never any such determination; also I reported of great treasure to be hid in *Hustreloe*, but it was as fabulous as the rest. I slew *Kyward*, and betrayed *Bellin;* I wounded the coney, and killed Dame *Sharp-beak*, the rook's wife. Lastly, I forgot at my last shrift one great deceit which I committed, but I will reveal it; and thus it was—

'As I went talking with the wolf between *Houthlust* and *Elverding*, we beheld a goodly bay mare grazing, with a black foal by her side, which was exceeding fat and wanton; the wolf at that instant was almost dead with hunger, insomuch that he entreated me to go to the mare, and know if she would sell her foal? I went and demanded the question. The mare said, "She would willingly sell it for money." I then asked the price? And she said, "The price was written in her hinder foot, which, if I pleased, I might come and read at my pleasure"; but I, that well understood her politic anger, said, "It is true that I cannot read, neither do I desire to buy your foal, only I am a messenger from the wolf, who hath a great desire to have it." "Then," said the mare, "let him come himself, and I will give him satisfaction."

'Then went I to the wolf, and told him what the mare said, assuring him that if he pleased, he might have his belly full of the foal, provided he could read, for the price was written in the mare's hinder foot. "Read," said the wolf, "what should ail me? I can, cousin, read Latin, French, English, and Dutch; I have studied in *Oxford*, and argued with many doctors; I have heard many stately plays, and sat in the place of judgment; I have taken degrees in both the laws, nor is there that writing which I cannot decipher."

'So desiring me to stay for him there, away he went to the mare, and craved that he might see and read the price of the foal; to which the mare consented, and lifting up her hinder foot, which was newly shod with strong iron and seven sharp nail heads, as the wolf looked thereon, she smote him just upon the forehead, so that she threw him over and over, and he lay in a dead swoon whilst a man might have ridden a mile and better, which done, away trotted the mare with her colt, and left the

poor wolf bloody and wounded, insomuch that
he howled like a dog.

' Then went I to him and said, " Sir *Isegrim*, dear uncle, how do you, have you eaten too much of the colt? Indeed, you are unkind, that will give me no part with you. I went your message honestly, methinks you have outslept your dinner; good uncle, tell me what was written under the mare's foot, was it in prose or rhyme? Indeed, I would fain know it; I think it was a prick song, for I heard you sing ; nay, you show your scholarship in all the arts."

' " Alas, *Reynard*, alas," said the wolf, " I pray you forbear to disdain me, for I am extremely wounded, and my anguish is so great that a heart of flint would pity me. The mare on her long leg hath an iron foot, and I took the nails to have been letters, on which I looked ; she hit me so full on the head that I think my skull is cloven."

' " Dear uncle," said I, " is this truth which you tell me? Believe it, you make me wonder ; why, I took you for one of the greatest clerks in this kingdom. Well, well, I perceive the old proverb is now made good in you : *The greatest clerks are not the wisest men*. Poor men sometimes may outstrip them in judgment, and the reason is, you great scholars study so much that you grow dull, in that you so much over-labour."

'And thus with these mocks and taunts I brought the wolf within a hair's-breadth of destruction.   And now, fair nephew, I have unladed my conscience, and delivered as many of my sins as I can call to my remembrance, wherefore, I beseech you, let me receive absolution and penance, and then come what chance shall at the court, I am armed against all dangers.'

Then *Grimbard* said, ' Your trespasses are great and heinous, nevertheless, who is dead must abide dead.   And therefore here I freely absolve you, upon assurance of your hearty repentance; only the contempt you made in sending him *Kyward's* head, and the abuse of so many falsehoods will lie heavy upon you.'

' Why,' said the fox, ' he that will live in the world to see this, hear that, and understand the third, must ever converse with affliction.   No man can touch honey but he must lick his fingers.   I often feel touches of repentance, but reason and our will are ever in continual combat, so that I often stand still as at my wits' end, and cry out against my sins, feeling a detestation of them.   But presently the world and her vanities appear to me again, and when I find so many stones and rubs in my way, and the examples of the crafty men of all degrees, to enchant me, I am forthwith taken again.

' The world fills me with covetousness, and the flesh with wantonness, so that losing my good resolutions, I am only for evil and wickedness. I hear their singing, piping, laughing, playing, and all kind of mirth, and I see their words and actions so contrary, that nothing is more uncertain and various; from them I learn my lying, and from lords' courts my flattery; for certainly lords, ladies, and clerks use most dissimulation.

' It is now an offence to tell great men truth; and he that cannot dissemble cannot live. I have oft heard men speak truth, yet they have still graced it with falsehood; for untruths many times happen into discourse unwillingly and without knowledge, yet having a handsome garment it ever goes for current. Dear nephew, it is now a fashion to lie, flatter, soothe, threaten, pray, and curse, and to do anything that may keep the weak in subjection; who does otherwise is held foolish. But he that cannot wimple falsehood in truth's kerchief, hath neither art nor cunning; but he that can do it, and deliver error without stammering, he may do wonders, he may wear scarlet, gray, or purple; he shall gain both by the laws spiritual and temporal, and write himself conqueror in every designment.

'There be many that imagine they can lie neatly, but their cunning oft fails them, so that when they think to feed of the fat morsels, they slip quite beside their trenchers. Others are blunt and foolish, and for want of method mar all their discourses; but he that can give to his lie a fit and an apt conclusion, can pronounce it without rattling, and make it as truth appear fair and amiable; that is the man, and worthy of admiration.

'But to speak truth is no cunning, it never makes the evil one laugh. To lie well and with a grace; to lift up wrong above right; to make mountains and build castles in the air; to make men juggle and look through their fingers, and all for the hope of gain only: this, nephew, is an art beyond expression; yet evermore of the end cometh misery and affliction. I will not deny but sometimes men may jest or lie in small things, for he that will speak all truths shall sometimes speak out of season.

To play *Placebo* may now and then be borne with; for whoso always speaks truth shall find many rubs in his way; men may err for need and mend it by counsel, since no trespass but hath his mercy, nor any wisdom but at some time dulleth.'

'Then,' said the brock, 'uncle, you are so wise you cannot fail in any purpose, and I would grow enamoured of you; your reasons so far surpass my understanding, that it is no need of your shrift, for yourself may play both the priest and confessor; you know the world in such sort, that it is impossible for any man to halt before you.'

With these and such manner of discourses they held on their journey towards the court; the fox's heart, for all his fair show, was sad and heavy, yet his countenance betrayed it not; but he passed without amazement through all the press of the court, even till he came to the presence of the King, and the brock marched close by his side, saying, ' Uncle, be not afraid, but be of good cheer; it is courage of whom fortune is ever enamoured.'

'Then,' said the fox, 'nephew, you say true, and your comfort avails me.'

And so on he went, casting a disdainful

countenance on those he liked not; or as one would say, Here I am, what is it that the proudest of you dare object against me? He beheld there many of his kin which he knew

loved him not, as the *Otter*, the *Beaver*, and divers others which I will name hereafter; and many he saw which loved him. As soon as he was come in the view of the King, he fell down humbly on his knee, and spake as followeth.

CHAPTER XIX

How Reynard *the Fox excused himself before the
King, and of the King's answer.*

'THAT divine power from whom nothing can
be hid, save my Lord the King, and my Lady
the Queen, and give them grace to know who
hath right and who hath wrong, for there
are many false shows in the world, and the
countenance bewrayeth not the heart. This
I wish were openly revealed, and that every
creature's trespass stood written on his forehead, albeit it cost me the uttermost of my
substance, or that you, my Sovereign Lord,
knew me as well as myself, and how I dispose
myself early and late, labouring in your service.
For which cause only malice makes all her
complaints against me, striving to thrust me
out of your grace and favour, insomuch that
out of my anguish I must needs cry shame
upon them which have so deadly belied me.

'Nevertheless, I know that you, my Lord and Sovereign Lady, are so excellent in your judgment, that you will not be carried away with falsehoods; and therefore I most humbly beseech your Majesties to take into your wisdom all things according to the right of your laws. For it is justice I look for, and desire that he which is found guilty may feel the weight of his punishment. For believe it, dread Lord, it shall be known before I depart from your court who I am, that I cannot flatter, but will show my face with an un-blemished forehead.'

All they that were in the presence stood amazed, and wondered when the fox spake so stoutly. But the King, with a stately countenance, said, '*Reynard*, I know you are expert in fallacies, but words are now too weak to relieve you. I believe this day will be the last of your glory and disgrace; for me, I will not chide you much, because I intend you shall live but a short time; the love you do bear me you have showed to the coney and the rook, and your requital shall be a short life on earth. The ancient saying is, *A pitcher may pass often to the water, but in the end it comes broken home.* And your evils

have so long succeeded, that they will now pay
you the hazard.'

At these words *Reynard* was stricken into

a great fear, and wished himself far away;
yet he bethought himself that now he must
bear through, what fortune soever came.
Whereupon he said, 'My Sovereign Lord

the King, it is but justice that you hear me answer my accusations, for were my faults more heinous than envy can make them, yet equity gives the accused leave ever to answer. I have with my counsel done you service in former times, and may no less still. I have never started from your Majesties, but walked by your side when others have gone from your presence; if then mine enemies with their slanders shall prevail against me, blame me not to complain. Time hath been it was otherwise, and mine may bring it to the old course, for the actions of good servants ought not to be forgotten.

'I see here divers of my kindred and friends which now make no value of me, whom I can prove go about to deprive you of the best servant you possess. Can your Majesty imagine if I had been guilty in the least imagined crime that I would thus voluntarily have made my appearance even in the throng of mine enemies? Oh, it had been too much indiscretion, nor would the liberty I had been so easily subjected. But Heaven be thanked I know mine innocence, and dare confront my worst enemy.

'Yet when my kinsman *Grimbard* first

brought me the tidings, I must confess I was half distracted with anger, and had I not been

in the censure of his church, I had appeared ere they had left complaining, but that detained me.   And I wandered with sorrow on the heath, till I met with my uncle *Martin*, the ape, who far exceedeth any priest in pastoral business, for he hath been attorney to the bishop of *Camerick* any time this nine years; and seeing me in this great agony of heart, he said, " Dear cousin, why are you thus heavy in spirit, and why is your countenance dejected ? Grief is easy to carry when the burden is divided amongst friends; for the nature of a true friend is to behold and relieve that which anguish will not suffer the oppressed to see or suffer."

'Then I answered him, "You say true, dear uncle, and the like is my fortune, for sorrow is without cause laid upon me, and of that I am not guilty; I am accused by those I ranked with my best friends : as namely, the coney, who came yesterday to my house as I was saying *Matins*, saying he was travelling towards the court, but was at that time both hungry and weary, and therefore requested of me some meat. I willingly consented, took him in and gave him a couple of manchets and sweet butter, for it was on Wednesday, on which day I never eat flesh. Besides, it was then a fast, by reason the feast of Whitsuntide was near. At which time we must have cleansed and prepared hearts, *Et vos estote parati*.

'" Now when he had almost well refreshed himself, my youngest son *Rossel* came in and offered to take away what he had left, for you know the nature of children is ever to be eating and craving; but presently the coney smote *Rossel* on the mouth, that his teeth bled, and the poor fool fell down almost in a swoon, which when *Reynardine*, my eldest son, beheld, he forthwith leaped to the coney, and caught him by the head, and questionless had slain him, had I not come to the rescue. Which done, I went and gave my son correction for his fault. But presently *Laprell* the coney posted to my Lord the King, and gave information that myself sought means to murder him. Thus I am accused without cause, and brought in danger, that in truth have best cause to accuse others.

'" But not long after came *Corbaut* the rook flying to my house with a sad noise. And demanding what he ailed? he answered, ' Alas, my wife is dead.' I craved the cause; he said, ' A dead hare lying on the heath full of maggots and vermin, of which she had eaten so much, that the worms had gnawed her throat in sunder'; and without speaking to me any more words, away he flew, leaving me much amazed; and now reports that I slew his wife, which how could I by any possible means do, considering she flieth in the air and I walk afoot on the ground? Thus, dear uncle, you see how I am slandered, but it may be it is for my old sins, and therefore I bear it with more patience."

'Then said the ape to me, "Nephew, you shall go to the court and disprove their falsehoods." "Alas, uncle," quoth I, "it cannot be, for the archdeacon hath put me in the Pope's curse, because I gave counsel to the wolf to forsake his holy orders, when he complained to me of his unableness to endure that strict life and much fasting; of which act I now much repent me, since he repayeth my love with nothing but hatred and malice; and with all the slanders he can invent, stirreth his Majesty daily against me. These things, dear uncle, bring me to my wits' end, for of necessity I must go to *Rome* for absolution; and in mine absence, what injury may happen to my wife and children through the malice of these bloody wretches, any one may guess. Whereas, on the other part, were I free of the Pope's curse, then I could go to the court, and plead mine own cause, and turn their malice into their own bosoms."

' Then said the ape, " Cousin, cast off your sorrow, for I know the way to *Rome* well, and am experienced in these businesses, for I am called the bishop's clerk, therefore I will go thither, and enter a plea against the archdeacon, and in spite of his will, bring you from the Pope a well-sealed absolution.

' " Tut, man, I have many great friends there, as mine uncle *Simon* and others, *Prentout*, *Waytescathe*, and the like, all which will stand unto me; besides, I will not go unfurnished of money, for I know praters are best heard with gifts, and the law hath no feet to walk on but money. A true friend is tried in necessity, and you shall find me without dissembling; therefore cast off your grief, and go to the court as soon as you can, for I will presently to *Rome*, and in the meantime, here I quit you of all your sins and offences, and only put them upon myself.

' " When you come to the court you shall find there Dame *Rukenaw* my wife, her two sisters, and my three children, with divers others of our family. I pray you salute them from me, and show them mine occasions; my wife is exceeding wise, and she shall find that her distressed friends shall not shrink when I can help them. I know she is faithful, and as behoves her will never leave her friend in danger. At the uttermost, if your oppression be more than you can bear, send presently to me to *Rome*, and not an enemy that you have, be it king or queen, or subject, even from the highest to the lowest, but I will presently put them in the Pope's curse, and send back such an interdiction, that no holy or sacred duty shall be performed till you have right and justice restored you.

' " This assure yourself I can easily perform, for his holiness is very old and little regarded, and only now cardinal *Paregold* beareth all the sway in the conclave, as being young, and rich in many friends; besides, he hath a favourite, of whom he is far enamoured, that he denies nothing she demandeth. His lady is my niece, and will do whatsoever I request her; therefore, cousin, go boldly to the King, and charge him to do you justice, which I know he will, since he understands the laws are made for the use of all men."

' This, my Sovereign Lord the King, when I heard him speak I smiled, and with great joy came hither to relate unto you the truth; therefore, if there be any creature within this court that can charge me with any trespass whatsoever, and prove it by testimony as the law requireth, or if otherwise, he will oppose himself against me, person to person, grant me but a day, and equal lists, and in combat I will maintain my innocence against him, provided he be equal to me in birth and degree; this law hath ever hitherto stood constant, and I

hope neither in me, for me, or by me, it shall now be broken.'

When all the assembly of beasts heard this, they were dumb and amazed to behold his stoutness. As for the coney and the rook, they were so scared they durst not speak, but privately stole away out of the court, and being far on the plain, they said, 'This devilish murderer hath such art in his falsehood, that no truth can look with better countenance,

which only ourselves know; but having no
other witness, therefore it is better we
depart than try combat with him, which is
so much too strong for us'; and so away they
went.

Isegrim the wolf, and *Bruin* the bear, were
very sad when they saw these two forsake the
court; whereupon the King said, 'If any will
appeal the fox, let him come forth, and he shall
be heard; yesterday we were laden with complaints, where are they to-day? Here is the
fox ready to answer.'

Then said the fox, 'My Sovereign Lord,
absence makes impudent accusers when
presence daunts them, as your highness may
see both by the coney and the rook. Oh, what
it is to trust the malice of these cowards, and
how soon they may confound good men; but
for me it matters not; nevertheless, had they,
at your Majesty's commandment, but asked me
forgiveness, I had quickly cast all their offences
behind me, for I will ever shake hands with
charity, and not hate or complain of mine
enemies; my revenge I leave to Heaven, and
justice to your Majesties.'

Then said the King, '*Reynard*, you speak
well, if the inward heart be like the outward

show, yet I fear your grief is not such as you express it.'

'It far surmounts it,' said the fox.

'No,' quoth the King, 'for I must charge you with one foul treason, which is, when I had pardoned all your great transgressions, and you had promised me to go a pilgrimage to the Holy Land; when I had furnished you with mail, state, and all things fitting that holy order; then in the greatest despite you sent me back in the mail by *Bellin* the ram the head of *Kyward* the hare, a thing so notoriously to my disgrace and dishonour, that no treason can be fouler. This you have no colour to deny, for *Bellin*, our chaplain, at his death revealed the whole process, and the same reward which he then gained, the same you shall receive, or else right shall fail me.'

At this sentence *Reynard* grew so sore afraid that he knew not what to say, but looked with a pitiable countenance upon all his kindred which stood round about him; his colour went and came, and his heart fainted, but none lent him either hand or foot to help him.

Then the King said, 'Thou dissembling and false traitor, why art thou now dumb?'

But the fox, being full of anguish, fetched a sigh as if his heart would have broken, so that every beast pitied him, save only the bear and the wolf, who much rejoiced to behold his sorrow.

CHAPTER XX

How Dame Rukenaw *answered for the Fox to the King, and of the parable she told.*

DAME *Rukenaw* the she ape, being aunt unto *Reynard*, and a great favourite of the Queen, was much grieved when she saw this distraction; and it was well for the fox that she was in the presence, for she was exceeding wise, and durst boldly speak; and therefore rising up, after reverence done, she said, 'My Lord the King, you ought not to be possessed with anger when you sit in judgment, for it becometh not nobility to be void of reason; it is discretion which should only accompany you in that reason; for my own part, I think I know the laws as well as some which wear furred gowns, for I have read many, and put some in use. It is well known I had ever in the Pope's palace a bed of straw, when other beasts lay on the bare ground, and I was ever suffered to speak freely

without interruption because I talk not beyond
mine experience.

'It is *Seneca's* opinion, that princes are
bound to do justice to all men, nor may the
law waver or halt with any partiality.   I do
not think but if every man which standeth
here should call to account all the actions of

his life, he could not choose but pity much the
state of my poor kinsman *Reynard*, and therefore I wish every one to know himself, for
none so sure but they may fall, and for him
that never erred, he is so good that he needeth
no amendment.   To do amiss and mend it by
counsel is humane and manly; but to trespass
and still gallop forward in iniquity is insuffer-

able. Goodness never forsaketh her own servants.

'This counsel would some take to their hearts, the day would not appear so dark as it doth to my cousin *Reynard*. It is well known that both his grandfather and father ever bore greater reputation in this court than either *Bruin* or *Isegrim*, or their whole generations. Alas! when have their counsels or wisdoms been worthy to have held comparison with those of my cousin *Reynard's?* Why, the passages of the world are to them prophecies which they understand not, and the court is turned topsy-turvy by his absence; the evil are now advanced and the good suppressed; but how this can long endure I see not, since the end of their labour is but the ruin of your Majesty.'

To this speech the King made this answer: 'Dame, had the fox done that offence to you that he hath done to others, your excuse would couch in another nature; you cannot blame me to hate him, since it is only he which breaketh my laws and covenants. You have heard him accused of theft, murder, and treason, how can you then defend him? If you will needs make him your saint, then set him upon the altar and do him worship; but believe it, there is no one good thing in him; and however you imagine, yet search him and you shall find him rotten and deformed. There is neither kinsman nor friend but yourself that will assist him, and therefore your violence draws my greater wonder. What companion hath he that ever thrived by his society, or whom hath he smiled on, that his tail hath not after dashed out the eye of?'

To this the she ape replied: 'My Lord, I love him, and have ever borne him a singular reverence, and I can well recount one noble and good action he did in your presence, for which then you thanked him, though it be now forgotten; yet the heaviest thing should ever weigh the most, and men should keep a measure in their affections, and not hate nor love with violence, since constancy is the greatest ornament of a princely nature. We should not praise the day till the evening come, nor is good counsel available but to those which mean to pursue it.

'I remember about some two years since there came to this court a man and a serpent, to have judgment in a doubtful controversy; for the serpent attempting to go through a hedge was taken by the neck with a snare, so that there was no way for him to escape with life. A certain man passing by, the serpent called and cried unto him and desired his help, or else he should perish presently. The man taking pity of him said, " If thou wilt faithfully promise me neither to do me hurt with thy tooth or tail, nor other poison about thee, I will release thee." The serpent presently swore " he would not, neither at that time nor any time hereafter "; so the man unloosed him and set him free, and they went forth and travelled together a long season.

'At the last the serpent grew exceeding hungry, and rushing upon the man offered to kill him; but the man started aside, and said, " What meanest thou to do? hast thou forgotten thine oath?" The serpent replied, " No; but I may justly kill thee since I am compelled thereto by hunger, which cancelleth all obligations." Then the man said, " If it be so, yet give me leave to live till we may meet with the next passenger which may judge the controversy."

'The serpent agreed thereto; so they travelled till they met with *Tisellin* the raven, and *Slinopere* his son, to whom relating the difference, the raven adjudged that the serpent should eat the man, hoping that he and his son should get a share also. But the man said, " How shall he that is a robber and lives by blood judge this cause? It must not be one but divers, and such as know both law and equity, that must judge this contention: the raven is neither just nor indifferent."

' Then they travelled till they met the bear and the wolf, unto whom also they told the matter, and they adjudged as against the man likewise. Then the serpent began to cast his venom at the man; but the man leaped away, and said, " You do me wrong thus to attempt to kill me "; and the serpent said, " Hath not the judgment gone twice on my side? " " Yes," said the man, " by such as are murderers themselves, and such as never keep promise; but I appeal unto the court, let me be tried by your King, and what judgment he giveth I will willingly abide."

' To this they all consented: so they came to the court before your Majesty, and the wolf's two children came with their father, the one was called *Empty-bell*, the other *Ever-full*, because they sought to devour the man. So the full process of the matter was declared to your Majesty; both the man's kindness and covenant, the serpent's danger and faith breach, occasioned through the extremity of hunger. Remember how much your highness was perplexed with their difference, and all your council also. For the man's sorrow, the serpent's hunger; the man's goodness, and the serpent's ingratitude, equally raised much pity in your bosom. But in the end such doubts rose that not any in your court was able to judge it.

'At last, when no help could be found, then you commanded my kinsman *Reynard* to decide the business. Then was he the oracle of the court, nor was anything received but what he propounded; but he told your Majesty it was impossible to give true judgment according to their relations; but if he might see the serpent in that manner as he was fettered, and the greatness of his danger, then he knew well how to give judgment therein. Then you commended him, and called him by the title of Lord *Reynard*, approving that to be done which he had spoken.

'Then went the man and the serpent to the place where the serpent was snared, and *Reynard* commanded the serpent to be fastened as before in the snickle, which being done,

then said your Majesty, " *Reynard*, what judgment will you now give?" and he replied,
" They are now, my Lord, in the same state
they were before at their first encounter:
they have neither won nor lost; therefore this
is my censure, if it be your Majesty's pleasure.
If the man will now loose and unbind the
serpent upon the same promise and oath made
formerly unto him, he may at his pleasure; but
if he think that hunger or other inconvenience
will make him break his faith, then may the
man go freely whither he will, and leave the
serpent bound and enthralled as he first found
him; for it is fit that ingratitude be so repaid."

' This judgment your Majesty then ap-
plauded for most excellent, and held the
wisdom of the fox unlimitable, terming him
the preserver of your honour. When did
ever the bear or wolf the like? They can howl
or scold, steal, rob, and eat fat morsels, make
their sides crack with others' ruin, and con-
demn him to death who takes a chicken; but
themselves which kill kine, oxen, and horses,
oh, they go safe and be accounted as wise as
Solomon, Avicenna, or *Aristotle*, and their deeds
and statutes must be read for monuments.
But if they come where virtue is to be exer-

cised, they are the first which retreat and let the simple go foremost, whilst they follow in the retreat with shame and cowardice.

'These, my Lord, and their like are the fools of the corrupt times, yet destroy towns, castles, lands, and people; nor care they whose house burneth so they may warm them by the fire; for it is their profit only at which their aim bendeth. But *Reynard* the fox and all his family have ever made the honour of the King their renown and advancement, and applied their counsel to do him service, not pride and boasting; this hath been and is his exercise, though it now be thankless. But time, I hope, will produce whose merit is greatest.

'Your Majesty says his kindred are all fallen from him, and start at his fortune; would any but your highness had affirmed it; you should then have seen there could not be a thing of greater falsehood. But your grace may say your pleasure, nor will I in any word oppose you, for to him that durst so do would both he and we bend our forces.

'It is known we dare fight, nor are we descended of any base generation; your highness may call to mind the worth of our pedigree, and how dearly from time to time they have respected him, willing ever to lay down their lives and goods for the safety of their noble kinsman *Reynard*. For mine own part I am one myself, and albeit I am the wife of another, yet for him I would not stick to spend my dearest blood. Besides, I have three full-grown children, which are known valiant and strong in arms, yet for his sake I would adventure them all to the uttermost peril. Albeit I love them with that dear affection that no mother doth exceed me. My first son is called *Bitelus* which is most active and nimble, my second, *Fulromp*, the third is a daughter called *Hatanet;* and these three are loving and dear to one another.'

With that she called them forth unto her, and said, 'Come, my dear children, and stand with your kinsman the noble *Reynard*, and with you come all the rest of our ancient family, and be all petitioners to the King, that he would do to *Reynard* the equity of his laws and kingdom.'

Then presently came forth a world of other beasts, as the squirrel and the ferret; for those love poultry as well as *Reynard* doth. Then came the otter and *Pantecrote* his wife, which I had almost forgotten, because in former time they had taken part with the bear against the fox, but now they dare not but obey Dame *Rukenaw*, for they stood in awe of her wisdom and greatness; and with these came above twenty other beasts for her sake and stood by *Reynard*. Then came also Dame *Atrot* and her two sisters, the weasel and ermine, the ass, the sow, the water-cat, and many others, to the number almost of a hundred, and stood by *Reynard* with such affection, as if his trouble did equally concern them.

Then said the ape, ' My Lord the King, now you may see that my kinsman hath friends which dare avow him, and we are your true and loyal subjects, which will never fail to do you faithful service. Therefore, let us with one voice beg of your Majesty, that *Reynard* may have justice; and if he be not able to disprove his adversaries, and clear the crimes imputed against him, let the law pass, for we will not murmur to see his destruction.'

Then said the Queen to *Rukenaw*, ' Thus much I told unto his Majesty yesterday, but his anger was so great he would not give ear to me.'

Also the leopard said, ' Sire, you must judge according to witness, for to be governed by will is tyrannous and ignoble.'

Then answered the King, ' It is true you inform me; but the disgrace done to my particular self in *Kyward's* death and other informations so robbed me of patience, that I had no leisure to look back either to law or reason. Therefore, now let the fox speak boldly, and if he can justly acquit himself of the crimes laid against him, I shall gladly restore him his liberty, and the rather for you his dear friends' sake, whom I have ever found faithful and loyal.'

Oh how infinitely glad was the fox when he heard these words, and said in himself, ' Thanks, my noble aunt, a thousand times, thou hast put me new blossoms on my dried roses, and set me in a fair path to liberty. I have one good foot to dance on; and I doubt not but to use my art of dissimulation so bravely, that this day shall be remembered for my renown and victory.'

CHAPTER XXI

How Reynard *excused himself of* Kyward's *death, and all other imputations, got the King's favour, and made a relation of certain Jewels.*

THEN spake *Reynard* the fox to the King, and said, 'Alas, my Sovereign Lord, what is that you said? Is good *Kyward* the hare dead? Oh where is then *Bellin* the ram, or what did he bring to your Majesty at his return? For it is certain I delivered him three rich and inestimable jewels, I would not for the wealth of *India* they should be detained from you; the chief of them I determined for you my Lord the King, and the other two for my Sovereign Lady the Queen.'

'But,' said the King, 'I received nothing but the head of poor murdered *Kyward*, for which I executed the ram, having confessed the deed to be done by his advice and counsel.'

'Is this true?' said the fox; 'then woe is me that ever I was born, for there are lost the goodliest jewels that ever were in the possession of any prince living; would I had died when you were thus defrauded; for I know it will be the death of my wife, nor will she ever henceforth esteem me.'

Then said the she ape, 'Dear nephew, why should you sorrow thus for transitory wealth? Let them go, only discourse what manner of jewels they were, it may be we shall find them again; if not, the magician M. *Alkarin* shall labour his books and search all the corners of the earth. Besides, whosoever detains them shall be cursed in all parishes till he restore them to the King's Majesty.'

'O aunt,' said the fox, 'do not persuade yourself so, for whosoever hath them will not restore them to gain an empire, they are so goodly and precious; yet your words do something appease me. But whom shall we trust in this corrupt age, when even sanctity itself walks masked and mistaken?'

And then fetching a deep sigh, with which he gilded his dissimulation, he proceeded on and said, 'Hearken all you of my stock and lineage, for I will here discover what these rich jewels were, of which both I and the King are defrauded. The first of them, and which indeed I intended for his Majesty, was a ring of fine and pure gold, and within this ring next the finger were engraven letters enamelled with azure and sables, containing three Hebrew names. For my own part, I could neither read nor spell them; but M. *Abrion* of *Trere*, the excellent linguist, who knoweth the natures of all manner of herbs, beasts, and minerals, to this famous Jew I showed the ring once, and he assured me that they were those three names which *Seth* brought out of Paradise when he brought to his father *Adam* the oil of mercy. And whosoever shall wear these three names about him shall never be hurt by thunder or lightning, neither shall any witchcraft have power over him; he shall not be tempted to do any sins, neither shall heat nor cold ever annoy him.

'Upon the top of the ring was encased a most precious stone of three several colours: the first like red crystal, and glittering like fire, and that with such brightness, that if one had occasion to journey by night, the

light thereof was so great as that at noon-
day; the other colour was white and clear,
as if it had been burnished, and the virtue
of it was to cure any blemish or soreness in
the eyes, or any part of the body; also by
stroking the place grieved therewithal, it
presently cured all manner of swellings,
headache, or any sickness whatsoever, whether
it were venom, weakness of stomach, colic,
stone, strangles, fistula, or canker, either
outwardly applied as aforeshown, or inwardly,
by steeping the stone in water, and then
drinking the same; the last colour was
green like grass mixed with a few small
spots of purple; and the learned affirmed for
truth, that whosoever wears this stone about
him could never be vanquished by his
enemies, and that no creature were he never
so strong and hardy, but he shall yield to
him, and he should be victor day and night
in all places.

'Again, as far as one bore it fasting, into
what company soever he chanced, albeit his
worst enemies, yet should he be of them
infinitely beloved, nor should any anger or
evil turn be remembered. Also, if one
should be naked in a vast wild field against

an hundred armed enemies, yet should not his heart fail him, but he should come off with honour and victory; only he must be nobly bred, and of no churlish disposition; for the ring gave no virtue to any which was not a true gentleman.   Now all these virtues considered, I thought myself unworthy to keep it, and therefore I sent it to you, my Lord the King, knowing you to be the most excellent of all creatures living, and one on whom all our lives depend, and therefore fittest to be guarded with so rich a jewel.

'This ring I found in my father's treasure, and in the same place also I found a comb and a glass mirror, which my wife desired of me; they were jewels of great wonder and admiration; these were sent to my lady the Queen, because of her grace and mercy extended towards me.

'To speak of the comb, it can never be too much praised, for it was made of the bone of a noble beast named *Panther*, which liveth between the great *India* and earthly *Paradise;* he is so goodly and fair of colour that there is no beautiful colour under heaven but some splendour thereof appears in him;

also the smell of him is delicately sweet and wholesome, that the very savour cureth all infirmities, and for his excellent beauty and rare odour all other beasts attend and follow him, for he is the physician to all their sicknesses.

'The *Panther* hath one fair bone broad and thin, which, whensoever this beast is slain, all the virtues of the whole beast do rest in that bone, which can never be broken, nor ever rot, consume or perish either by fire, water, or other violence, yet it is so light a small feather may poise it. The smell of it hath that virtue, that whosoever smells it, taketh delight in no other thing whatsoever, and they are presently eased of all manner of diseases and infirmities, and the heart is cheerful and merry ever after.

'This comb is polished like unto fine silver, and the teeth of it are small and straight, and between the great teeth and the small in a large field or space, there is graven many an image, subtilely made, and cunningly enamelled about with fine gold; the field is checked with sables and silver, and enamelled with cybor and azure; and therein is contained the story how *Venus*, *Juno*, and *Pallas* strove for the golden ball in the mountain *Ida*, and how it was put to *Paris*, to give it to the fairest of them.

'Now for the glass mirror, it was not inferior to either of the other; for the glass which stood thereon was of such virtue that men might see and perceive therein whatsoever was done within a mile thereof, whether it were the actions of men, or beasts, or anything else the owner would desire to know, and whosoever but gazed therein, if he had any malady whatsoever, it was presently cured. So great were the virtues of this rare glass, that wonder not if I shed tears to think of the loss; for the wood in which this glass stood was light and fast, and is called *catine*, it will last for ever; for no worms, dust, wet, or time can consume it; and therefore King *Solomon* ceiled his temple with the same. The value exceeds far the value of gold; it is like to the wood *hebenus*, of which King *Crampart* made a horse, for the love of the most beautiful daughter of King *Morcadiges*.

'This horse was made with such art within, that whosoever rode on it, if he pleased, he would run above an hundred miles in less than an hour, which was approved by *Clamades*

the King's son, who not believing in the
engine, and being young and lusty, leaped
upon the horse, and presently *Crampart* turning
a pin that stood in the breast of the engine,

moved and went out of the palace through the
windows, and in the first minute he was gone at
least ten miles. *Clamades* was much affrighted
at the wonder, and imagined, as the story said,
that he should never have returned back
again; but of his long journey, much fear,

great trouble, and infinite joy, when he had learned to manage and govern the wooden beast, I leave to speak for tediousness' sake, only the high virtue of all issued from the wood.

'Of this wood the glass case was made, being larger than the glass by half a foot and more square, upon which verge was deciphered divers many strange histories in gold, in silver, in sables, yellow, azure, and cynope; and these colours were very curiously wrought and inter-laid together, and under each history the words so engraven and enamelled, that any man might read the whole story.

'Believe it, the world never produced a thing of greater worth, lustre, or pleasure. In the upper part thereof stood a horse in his natural glory, fat, fair, and fiery, which braved a stately hart which ran before him; but seeing he could not overtake the hart in swiftness, at which he infinitely disdained, he went to a herdsman standing by, and told him, if he would help him to take a hart which he would show him, he should have all the profit of the conquest, as the horns, skin, and flesh.

'Then the herdsman asked him what means he should use to get him. The horse said, "Mount upon my back, and I will bear thee after him, till with tiring we take him." The herdsman took his offer, and bestriding the horse followed the deer; but he fled away so fast, and got so much ground of the horse, that with much labour the horse grew weary, and he bade the herdsman alight, for he would rest himself awhile. But the herdsman said, "I have a bridle on thy head, and spurs on my heels, therefore know thou art now my servant, neither will I part with thee, but govern thee as seems best to my pleasure." Thus the horse brought himself into thraldom and was taken in his own net, for no creature hath a greater adversary than his own envy, and many which labour the hurt of others, still fall upon their own ruin.

'In another part were figured an ass and a hound, which were both the servants of a rich man. This man loved his hound exceedingly, and would oft play with him, and suffer the dog to fawn and leap upon him, and now and then to lick him about the mouth. Now when *Baldwin* the ass saw this, he began to envy the hound, and said, "What sees my master in this foul hound, that he suffers him thus to leap upon him and kiss him? I see no profitable service he doth him. I labour, bear and draw, and do more service in one week than the dog and his whole kind are able to do in a year, and yet have I not the tithe of his favours; for he sitteth by his trencher, eats the fat of his meat, and lies on carpets and pillows; when I that do all am fed only with nettles and thistles. Well, I will no longer endure it, but I will study to have my lord's favour as much as the hound, if not in greater measure."

' Anon, the master of the house came home, and the ass lifting up his tail leaped with his forefeet on his shoulders, and braying and grinning, and put forth his mouth to kiss him, and used such rude unmannerly action, that he rubbed all the skin from his master's ear, and almost overthrew him, so that the man was forced to cry out, " Help, help, for this ass will kill me." Then came in his servants with staves, and beat the ass so exceedingly, that he was almost slain, which done, he returned to his stall again, and was an ass as he was before. In the same manner, they which do envy and spite at others' welfare, if they receive the same reward, it is nothing more than is due to their merit; for an ass is an ass and was born to eat thistles; and where asses govern, there order is never observed, for they have no eye either on this side, or beyond their own private profit; yet sometimes they are advanced, the more is the pity.

'In another part was figured the story how my father and *Tibert* the cat travelled together, and had sworn by their troth that neither for love nor hate they would depart one from the other; but it happened on a time they saw hunters coming over the fields with a kennel of hounds, from which they fled apace, for their lives were in danger.   Then said the fox, "*Tibert*, whither shall we fly? for the hunters have espied us; for mine own part, I have a thousand wiles to escape them, and as long as we abide together we shall not need to fear them."

'But the cat began to sigh, and was exceedingly afraid, and said, "*Reynard*, what needs many words? I have but one wile, and that must help me"; and forthwith he clambered up to the top of a high tree, where he lurked amongst the leaves, that neither huntsman nor hound could hurt him, and left my father to abide the whole hazard, for the whole kennel pursued him, horns and halloos echoing after him, " Kill the fox, kill the fox."

'This when *Tibert* saw, he mocked my father, and said, " Now, cousin *Reynard*, it is time to let loose all your wiles, for if your wit fail you, I fear your whole body will perish." This my father hearing from him he most trusted, and being then in the height of pursuit, wearied and almost spent, he let his mail slip from his shoulders, to make himself so much lighter; yet all availed not, for the hounds were so swift they had caught him, had he not by chance espied a hole, into which he entered, and escaped the hounds and huntsmen.

'Thus you may see the false faith of the cat, whose like there be many living at this time, and though this might well excuse me from loving the cat, yet my soul's health and charity bind me to the contrary, and I wish him no hurt, though his misfortunes shall never be grievous to me; not so much for hatred as the remembrance of his injuries, which often contends against my reason.

'Also in that mirror stands another history of the wolf, how on a time he found upon a heath a dead horse, whose flesh being eaten away, he

was fain to gnaw and devour the bones, which he did with such greediness, that swallowing them too hastily down, one fell so across his throat that he was almost choked, and hardly escaped with life; whereupon he sought every place for the cunningest surgeons, promising them great gifts to ease his torment; but having lost much labour, in the end he met with the crane, and besought him with his long neck and bill to help him, and he would highly reward him.

'The crane, greedy of gain, put his head into the wolf's throat, and brought out the bone. The wolf started at the pull, and cried out aloud, "Thou hurtest me; but I do forgive thee; yet do it not again I charge thee, for at another's hands I would not bear it."

'Then the crane said, "Sir *Isegrim*, go and be frolic, for you are whole. I look for no more but the reward you promised me."

'"How," said the wolf, "what impudence is this? I suffer and have cause to complain; yet he will be rewarded, he will not so much as thank me for his life, but forgets that his head was in my mouth, and how I suffered him to draw it out again without hurting; albeit he has put me to exceeding much pain. I suppose it is I which deserve the reward, and not the crane."

' Thus you may see the fashion of ungrateful men in these days, how ever they reward good with evil; for whereas pride is exalted, there honour is ever laid in the dust. There be in the world which ought to reward and do good to those that have advanced them, which now complain, and make those advancements in-juries; but the guerdon will follow; for it is the wisest counsel, that whosoever will go about to chastise another, should ever be sure of his own clearness.

' All this and a world more than I can well remember was curiously wrought on this glass; for the work-master thereof was the most cunning and profound clerk in all sciences that ever breathed. And because the jewels were too good and precious for me to keep, therefore I sent them to the King and Queen's Majesties as a present to witness my faith and service. Oh, he that had seen what sorrow my children made when I sent the glass away, would have wondered! for by reason of the great virtue therein, they oft gazed in the same, both to behold themselves, and to see how their clothing and apparel became them.

' Little did I then imagine that good *Kyward* was so near his death, for except himself, and *Bellin* the ram, I knew no messengers worthy to carry so rich a present. But I will search the whole world, and I will find the murderer, for murder cannot be hid. It may be, he is in this presence which knows what is become of *Kyward*, albeit he do conceal it ; for the wicked walk like saints.

' Yet the greatest wonder of all is, which troubled me most, that my Lord the King should say, that my father nor myself ever did good. But the troubles of affairs may well breed forgetfulness in Kings, otherwise your Majesty might call to mind how, when the King your father lived, and you were a prince not above two years old, my father came from the school at *Mountpeloir*, where he had studied five years the art of physic, and was expert in all the principles thereof, and so famous in those days, that he wore clothes of silk and a golden girdle. Now when he was come to the court, he found the King in great extremity of sickness, which was no little grief unto him, for he loved the King most dearly, and the King rejoiced at his sight, and would not suffer him to be out of his presence. All others might walk whither they would, only he must ever be near him. Then said your father, "*Reynard*, I am exceeding sick, and I feel my sickness increasing." My father answered, "My lord, let me feel your pulse, and as soon as I perceive your state, I will give my opinion." The King did as he was advised,

for he trusted not any equal with him. Then said my father, "My best Lord, if you will be eased of your grief, you must needs eat the liver of a wolf of seven years old, or else your disease is incurable."

'The wolf at that time stood by your father, but said nothing; whereupon the King said, "Sir *Isegrim*, you hear how there is nothing which can cure me but your liver." The wolf replied, "Not so, my Lord, for I am not yet full five years old." "It is no matter," answered my father, "let him be opened, and when I see the liver, I will tell you if it be medicinal." Then was the wolf carried to the kitchen and his liver taken out, which the King ate, and was presently cured of his sickness.

'Then the King thanked my father, and commanded all his subjects, on pain of death, from thenceforth to call him Master *Reynard*. So he abode still about the King, walked by his side, and was trusted in all things; and the King gave him, for an honour, a garland of roses, which he must ever wear upon his head. But these remembrances are all lost and gone, and his enemies are now only advanced; virtue is put back, and innocence lives in sorrow; for when baseness and covetousness are made commanders, they neither know themselves, nor look at the lowness from whence they are risen. They have no hearts for pity, nor ears for the poor man's cause. Gold is the goal they run to, and gifts the god which they worship. What great man's gate doth not now lock up covetousness? Where is not flattery entertained, and what prince takes hate at his own praises? But should greatness need their honest service, well might they starve ere they could gain that employment; for like wolves they had rather see their masters die than lend them the least part of their liver.

'This, my Lord, was an accident which fell in your youth, and you may well forget it; yet, without boasting, I myself may say I have done to you both honour and service, and you haply also forget this which I shall repeat, which I vow I do not to upbraid your Majesty, for you are ever worthy of more than I can tender; and my uttermost is but the rent of a loyal subject, which I am ever bound by the laws of God and nature to perform.

'So it was, that on a time *Isegrim* the wolf and I had gotten a swine under us, and by reason of his extreme loud crying, we were compelled to bite him to death. At which time yourself came out of a grove unto us, and saluted us friendly, saying, "That you and the Queen your wife, who came after you, were both exceeding hungry, and entreated us to give you part of our getting."

'*Isegrim* then whispered in such manner that none could understand him; but I spake out aloud, "With all my heart, my Lord, and were it better than it is, it were too mean for your service." But *Isegrim*, according to his wont, departed grumbling, and took half of the swine, giving you and the Queen but one poor quarter, the other he himself unmannerly devoured, and left me for my share but poor half of the lungs. When your Majesty had eaten

your part, you were still hungry, but the wolf would deliver none; so that you reached him a blow with your foot, which tore all the skin from about his ears, so that he ran away crying and howling with all extremity. But your Majesty commanded him to return again speedily and bring you more meat; yet he went away grumbling. Then I besought your Majesty that I might go with him: and I well remember your answer. So away we went together, his ears dropping blood all the way as he went.

'In the end we took a calf, and when your Majesty saw us bring it, you laughed, and said to me, " I was a swift huntsman, and could find my game quickly, and therefore I was fit to serve in time of necessity." Then you bade me to divide it, and I did it, and gave one half thereof to your Majesty, the other half to the Queen. As for the liver, lungs, and all the inwards, I sent them to the young princes your children. As for the head, I gave it to *Isegrim* the wolf, and took unto myself but the feet only. Then said your Majesty, " Ah, *Reynard*, who taught you to make these courteous divisions?" " My Lord," answered I, " that did this priest which sits here with the bloody pate; for he lost his skin for his too much inequality, and for his covetousness hath reaped nothing but shame and dishonour. But it matters not, for there be many wolves in these days that would even eat up their best friends and kindred—nay, if they had power, even your Majesty also, for they make no respect either of friend or enemy. But woe to that commonwealth where such have the upper hand and government."

'My gracious Lord, this and many such like
actions as this have I done for your Majesty,
which were it not for tediousness' sake I could
well repeat. But they are all now cast out of
your remembrance; time and my loyalty I
hope will one day again recall them. I have
seen the day when no matter was finished in
the court without my advice and censure,
though now that judgment is not so reputed;
yet it may be, the same reputation may spring
up again, and be believed as firmly as before,
as long as it swerves not from justice, which is
the only thing I aim at. For if any one can
charge me otherwise and prove it by witness,
here I stand to endure the uttermost the law
can inflict upon me; but if malice only slander
me without witness, I crave the combat according to the law and instance of the court.'

Then said the King, '*Reynard*, you say
well, nor know I anything more of *Kyward's*
death than the bringing of his head unto me
by *Bellin* the ram, therefore of it I here acquit
you.'

'My dear Lord,' said the fox, 'I humbly
thank you: yet is his death so grievous unto
me I cannot let it pass so easily. I remember
my heart was heavy at his departure, and I was

ready to sink to the ground, which was a certain presage of the loss which happened.'

These words, and the sad looks of the fox, so amazed all the beholders, that they could not choose but believe all that he uttered, so that every one bemoaned his loss, and pitied his sorrow. But the King and Queen were most touched with the same, and then entreated him that he would make diligent search for the finding of them out, for his praises had stricken them far in love with the jewels. And because he told them he had sent those jewels unto them, though they never saw them, yet they gave him as great thanks as if they had been in their safe possession, and desired him he would be a means they might be restored to them again.

CHAPTER XXII

How Reynard *made his peace with the King, and how* Isegrim *the Wolf complained of him again.*

THE fox understood their meaning exceeding well, and though he little meant to perform what they entreated, yet he thanked the King and Queen for the comforts they gave him in his great extremity. He vowed not to rest, neither night nor day, but to search all the corners of the earth till he had found what was become of those jewels. Also he entreated his Majesty, that if they should be concealed in such places where he might be withstood by force, so as neither his prayers nor power might attain unto them, that then his highness would assist him both because it was an occasion which concerned him so nearly, and also a thing required from his office, being an act of perfect justice, to punish theft and murder, both which were contained in this action.

Then the King assured him that so soon as it should be known where they were, no help or assistance should be wanting. The fox gave the King humble thanks, for now he had gotten all his purposes to the wished end he expected, and by his false tale and flattery had so fastened the King unto him, that now he might go freely whither he pleased, and none should dare to complain of him.

Only *Isegrim* the wolf stood all this while infinitely displeased, and not able to contain his anger any longer, he said, ' O my Lord the King, is it possible your Majesty should be so much childish or weak of belief as to fix your trust upon the falsehood of this ever-deceiving merchant, which hath nothing but shadows and chimeras wherewith to enchant you? Oh be not so easily seduced; he is a wretch all covered and besmeared with murder and treason, and even to your own face hath made a scoff of your Majesty. For my own part I am glad he is here in your presence, and I intend to ring him such a peal of contrary nature, that all the lies he can invent shall not bear him away with safety.

' So it is, my dread Lord, that this dissembling and false traitor not long since did betray my wife most shamefully; for it happened upon a winter's day, that they two travelled together through a very great water, and he persuaded my wife that he would teach her a singular art, how to catch fish with her tail, by letting it hang angle-wise in the water a good while, whereunto, he said, there would so much fish instantly cleave, that half a dozen of them should not be able to devour it.

'The silly fool, my wife, supposing all to be truth which came from him, went presently into the mire up to the middle before she came to the water, and coming into the depth of the water, as he directed her, she held her tail down still in the water, expecting when there the fish would cleave to it; but the weather being sharp and frosty, she stood there so long that her tail was frozen hard to the ice, so that all the force she had was not able to pull it out. This no impudence can make him deny, for I came and saw him there. Oh how much jealousy, grief, and fury assailed me at that instant, I was even distracted to behold them; and I cried, "*Reynard*, villain, what art thou doing?" but he seeing me so near approaching, presently ran his way.

'So I went unto her with much sorrow and

heaviness, having a world of labour ere I could break the ice about her; and in spite of all my cunning, yet she was compelled to leave a piece of her tail behind her: and indeed we both hardly escaped with our lives. For by reason of the great anguish she endured, she barked so loud, that the people of the next village rose up, and came with staves and bills, with flails and pitchforks, and the wives with their distaves, and so fiercely assaulted us, crying Kill, kill, and Slay, slay, that I was never in so desperate a taking. One slave amongst the rest, which was strong and swift of foot, hurt us sore with a pikestaff; and had not the night befriended us, we had never escaped the danger. From hence we came into a field full of brooms and brambles, where we hid us from the fury of our enemies.

'Thus, my gracious Lord, you have heard how this traitor and murderer hath used us, and against the same we crave the right of your law and justice.'

But *Reynard* answered and said, 'If this were true, I confess it would touch me near in honour and reputation; but it is not possible that such a slander should be proved against me: I confess I taught her to catch fish, and

taught her how to enter the water and never touch the mire; but her greediness so transported her when she heard me name the fish, that she ran without respect of any path or direction, and so coming into the ice, she was there presently frozen by reason of her too long tarrying, for she had more fish than would have satisfied twenty reasonable appetites. But it is commonly seen that who all would have, all forego, for covetousness seldom bringeth anything well home; yet when I saw her so fastened in the ice, I used all my best endeavours to loosen her, and so indeed was heaving and shoving about her, but to little purpose, for by reason of her weight I was not able to move her.

'Now whilst this was doing, came *Isegrim*, and seeing me so busy about her, churl-like he most vilely slandered me, and threatened much vengeance against me, so that more to eschew his blasphemy than fury I went my way, and he came, and with as great ado, and as much heave and shove he helped her out; which done, they then almost starved with cold, ran and skipped up and down the fields to get them heat: and that this is all truth which I have spoken, I will willingly be deposed, for I would not be the father of any falsehood before your Majesty, to be master of many millions; however my fortunes go, I respect not, truth is my badge, and hath ever been the ensign of all my ancestors; and if there be any scruple or doubt made of mine assertion, I ask but eight days' liberty, that I may confer with my learned counsel, and I will so approve all my words by the oath and testimony of good and sufficient witness, that your Majesty and your honourable council shall accord to the justness of my protestation.

'As for the wolf, what have I to do with him? it is well known already that he is a debauched and almost notorious villain, false both to heaven and to your Majesty; and now his own words witness him a base slanderer of women, therefore I refer myself to the trial of his wife; if she accuse me, let the world hold me guilty, provided she may be made free from her husband, whose tyranny will compel her to say anything, though never so unjustly.'

At this forth stepped Dame *Ereswine*, the wolf's wife, and said, 'O *Reynard*, thou hast so oily a smooth tongue, and so dipped in flattery, that no man is safe from thine enchantment; it is not once, but oft thou hast deceived me;

remember but how thou didst use me at the
well with two buckets,
hanging at one cord, and
running through one
pulley, which ever as one
went down the other
went up.   I remember
how thou getting into one
of them, fell down into
the bottom of the well,
and there sat in great
danger and peril, so that
I ran thither with great
haste, and heard thee sigh
and make great moan;
then asking thee how
thou camest there, thou
answeredst me that thou
wert there a-fishing, and
hadst much fish, of which
thou hadst eaten so many
that you were ready to
break with swelling.

   'Then I asked how I
might come to thee, and
thou saidst, "Aunt, leap
into that bucket which

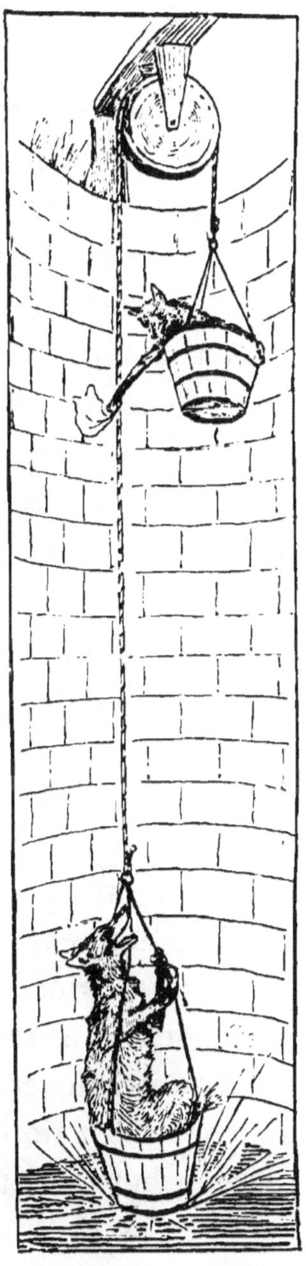

hangeth there, and you will be presently with me"; which I no sooner did, but being much heavier than thyself, I fell presently to the bottom of the well, and thou came up to the top; at which when I seemed to be angry, thou said, "Aunt, this is but the fashion of the world; ever as one comes up another must go down"; and so said, you leaped out of the bucket and ran your way, leaving me there all alone, where I remained a whole day, pined with hunger and starved with cold; and ere I could get out from thence, received so many blows, that my life was never in greater danger.'

The fox replied, 'Aunt, though the strokes were painful unto you, yet I had rather you should have them than myself, for you are stronger and better able to bear them; and at that time of necessity, one of us could not escape them: besides, aunt, I taught you wisdom and experience, that you should not trust either friend or foe, when the matter he persuades to is the avoiding of his own peril; for nature teacheth us to love our own welfare, and he which doth otherwise is crowned with nothing but the title of folly.'

Then said Sir *Isegrim* to the King, 'I

beseech your Majesty mark how this dissembler
can blow with all winds, and paint his mischief
with false colours: a world of times hath he
brought me into these hazards. Once he
betrayed me to his aunt the she ape, where
ere I escaped I was fain to leave one of mine
ears behind me. If the fox dare tell the
truth of the story, for I know his memory
to be much better, besides he is apt to
catch advantage from the weakness of my
language, I desire no better evidence against
him.'

Then said the fox, 'Willingly I will do it,
and without flattery or falsehood; and therefore I beseech your Majesty lend me your
royal patience. Upon a certain time the wolf
here came to me into the wood, and complained
unto me that he was exceeding hungry, yet I
never saw him fuller in my life; but he would
ever dissemble. At which presently I took
pity on him, and said I was also as hungry as
he: so away we went and travelled half a day
together without finding anything.

'Then began he to whine and cry, and said
he was able to go no farther. Then hard by
the foot of a hawthorn tree we espied a hole all
covered over with brambles, and heard a great

rushing therein, but could not imagine the cause why: then I desired the wolf to go in, and look if anything were there to profit us, for something I knew there was. Then said he, " Cousin, I would not creep into the hole for a hundred pounds, till I knew certainly what was therein ; for there may be danger: but if you please to attempt it, who I know hath both art and wit to save yourself, I will stay here under this tree till you return ; but I beseech you make haste and let me know what is therein as soon as you perceive it."

' Behold, my dread Lord the King, thus he hath made me, poor silly beast, to go before into the hazard, and he who is great, strong, and mighty did abide without in peace, wherein I expressed no little friendship, for I would not endure the like danger for a kingdom. But to proceed : I entered into the hole, and found the way dark, long, and tedious; in the end I espied a great light, which came in on the farther side of the hole, by which I saw there lying a great she ape, with eyes glimmering and sparkling with fire, her mouth set round with long sharp teeth, and on her hands and feet nails sharp as an elfin or bodkin. I imagined her at first a marmoset or baboon,

or else a mercat, for a more dreadful beast I
never beheld in all my lifetime, and by her
side lay divers of her children, which like
herself were stern and cruel of countenance:
when they saw me come towards them, they
gaped wide with their mouths upon me, so
that I grew amazed, and wished myself far
from the harbour.

'But resolving with myself that now I was
in I must quit myself as well as I could, I
looked more constantly upon her, and methought she appeared bigger than *Isegrim* the
wolf, and the least of her brats much larger
than myself; a fouler company I never saw,
they were all laid in so bad litter, that I was
almost poisoned with the place. For my own
part I durst not but speak them fair, and
therefore I said, " Aunt, God give you many
good days, and bless you and my cousins,
your pretty children ; questionless they are
the fairest of their ages that ever I beheld,
and so surpass in beauty and perfection that
they may well be accounted of most princely
issue. Truly, aunt, we are infinitely beholden
to you that doth add this increase and glory
to your family. For mine own part, dear aunt,
when I heard you were laid down and indis-

posed, I could not stay but must needs come to visit you."

'Then replied she, "Cousin *Reynard*, you are exceeding welcome; you have found me like a slut, but I thank you for your kind visitation: you are a worthy gentleman, and through the King's dominions, for your wit and judgment, held of singular reputation, you do much honour to our kindred, and are famous for the means you work to their preferment. I must entreat you to take the charge of my children, and instruct them in the rules of knowledge and science, that they may know hereafter how to live in the world. I have thought of you ever since they were born, and resolved upon this, cousin, because I knew your perfection, and that you accompanied yourself with none but the good and the virtuous."

'Oh how glad was I when I heard those words to proceed from her, which kindness was only because at first I called her aunt, who indeed was no soul kin unto me; for my true aunt indeed is only Dame *Rukenaw*, who standeth yonder, who indeed is the mother of excellent children. Yet, notwithstanding, I answered this foul monster: "Aunt, my life

and goods are both at your service, and what
I can do for you, night or day, shall ever be
at your command and your children's."

'Yet I most heartily wished myself far
from them at that instant, for I was almost
poisoned with their smell. And I pitied
Isegrim who was sore griped with hunger all
this while; and offering to take my leave, and
feigning that my wife would think it long till
my return, she said, " Dear cousin, you shall
not depart till you have eaten something. I
shall take it unkindly if you offer it"; then
rose she up, and carried me into an inner
room, where was great store of all kind of
venison, both of the red deer, fallow deer, and
roe; and great store of partridges, pheasants,
and other fowls, that I was amazed much from
whence such store of meat should come.

'Now when I had eaten sufficiently, she
gave me a side and half a haunch of a hind,
to carry home to my wife, which I was ashamed
to take, but that she compelled me; and so
taking my leave, and being entreated often to
visit her, I did depart thence, much rejoiced
that I had sped so well.

'Now being come out of the causey, I spied
where *Isegrim* lay groaning pitifully, and I

asked him how he fared? He said, " Wondrous ill, and so extremely ill, that, dear nephew, without some meat I die presently": then did I take compassion on him, and gave him my wife's token, which preserved his life, and for which then he gave me a world of thanks, though now he hates me extremely.

' But as soon as he had devoured up my venison, he said, " *Reynard*, my dear cousin, what found you in the hole? believe it, I am now more hungry than I was before, and this small morsel hath but sharpened my teeth to eat more." Then said I to him, " Uncle, get you into that hole, and you shall find store of victuals, for there lieth my aunt with her children : if you can flatter and speak her fair, you need fear no hard measure, all things will be as you would wish it."

' I think, my gracious Lord, this was warning sufficient, and that which might have armed any wise spirit ; but rude and barbarous beasts will never understand wisdom, and therefore they loathe the policies they know not. But yet he promised to follow my counsel ; so forth he went into that foul dismal hole, and found the ape in that filthy sort as before I described ; which when he saw, being affrighted, he cried out, " Woe and alas, I think I am come into evil; did ever creature see such fearful goblins? Drown them, for shame drown them, they are so ugly, they will scare all the world; why, they make my hair stand on end with their horrid deformity."

'Then said she, " Sir *Isegrim*, their creation is not my fault, let it suffice, they are my children, and I am their mother; nor ought their beauty or hard favour to displease you: there was a kinsman of theirs here to-day, and is but newly departed, who is well known to exceed you, both in birth, virtue, and wisdom, and he accounted them fair and lovely; for your opinion I care not, therefore you may depart at your pleasure."

'Then he replied, " Dame, I would have you know that I would eat of your meat, it is much better bestowed on me than on those ugly urchins." But she told him, " she had no meat." " Yes," said he, " here is meat enough," and with that, offering to reach at the meat, my aunt started up with her children, and ran at him with their sharp nails, and so clawed him, that the blood ran about his ears, and I heard him cry and howl so extremely, that it appeared he had no defence but to run out of the hole as fast as he could.   For indeed he came out both extremely beaten, and extremely bitten, and all his skin slashed like a Spanish jerkin ; and one ear left behind as a pawn of his manners.

'This when I saw, I asked him if he had flattered sufficiently? and he said he had spoken as he found, for the dame was a foul animal, and the litter most ugly monsters. Then I told him, how he should have commended their beauties, and taken them for his best of alliance.   And he replied, he had rather have seen them all hanged.   "Then," quoth I, "you must always receive such reward as now you do, but wisdom would do otherwise ; fair words never come out of season, and better than we hold it for a rule worthy imitation."

'Thus, my Lord, I have told you truly how he came by his red nightcap, which I know he cannot, nor dare not deny, for all is true without any addition.'

CHAPTER XXIII

How Isegrim *proffered his glove to* Reynard *to fight with him, which* Reynard *accepted, and how* Rukenaw *advised the* Fox *how to carry himself in the fight.*

THE wolf answered the fox, 'I may well forbear, false villain as thou art, thy mocks and scorns; but thine injuries I will not. You say I was almost dead for hunger, when you helped me in my need: but thou liest falsely therein, for it was nothing but a bare bone thou gavest me, when thou hadst gnawed all the meat thereof; and therefore know in this thou injurest my reputation. Again, thou accusest me of treason against the King, and to conspire his Majesty's death, for certain treasure thou sayest is in *Hustreloc:* also thou hast abused and slandered my wife, which will ever be an infamy to her name if it be not revenged.

'These things considered, I have forborne you long, therefore now look not to escape; wherefore seeing there is no other testimony but our own consciences, here before you, my Lord the King, and the rest of my noble lords, friends, and alliances, here I affirm and will approve to the last drop of my blood that thou, *Reynard* the fox, art a false traitor and a murderer; and this I will approve and make good upon thy body within the lists of the field, body against body, by which means our strife shall have an end, and in witness whereof I cast thee here my glove, which I dare thee to take up, that I may have right for mine injuries, or else die like a recreant.'

Reynard was something perplexed when he saw this, for he knew himself much too weak for the wolf, and feared to come by the worst; but straight remembering the advantage he had, by reason that the wolf's fore-claws were pulled away and that they were not yet fully cured, he said, 'Whosoever he be that saith I am a traitor or a murderer I say he lieth in his throat, especially *Isegrim* above all others; poor fool, thou bringest me to the place I desire, and to the purpose I wish for, in sign whereof I take up the gage, and throw

down mine, to approve all thy words lies and
falsehoods.'

This said, the King received their pledges,
and admitted the battle, commanding them to
put in their sureties, that the next morrow

they should try the combat: then stepped
forth the bear and the cat, and were sureties
for the wolf; and for the fox were sureties
Grimbard the brock and *Bitelus*. When all
ceremonies were finished, the she ape took
Reynard aside, and said, ' Nephew, I beseech
you take care of yourself in this battle, be bold

and wise.   Your uncle taught me once a prayer of singular virtue for him which was to fight; and he learned it of that excellent scholar and clerk, the abbot of *Budelo*, and he that saith this prayer with a good devotion fasting, shall never be overcome in combat, and therefore, my best nephew, be not afraid, for to-morrow I will read it over to you, and the wolf shall never prevail against you.'

The fox gave her many thanks for her favours, and told her his quarrel was good and honest, and therefore he had no doubt of happy success; so all that night he rested with his kinsfolk about him, who drove away the time with pleasant discourse.   But Dame *Rukenaw*, his aunt, still beat her brain how to work him advantage in the combat, wherefore she caused all his hair to be shaven off, even from his head to the tail, and then she anointed all his body quite over with oil of olive, so that she made it so smooth and slippery that the wolf could catch no hold of him.   Besides he was round, fat and plump of body, which much availed to his advantage; then she advised him, ' At these especial times keep your tail as close as can be between your legs, lest he catch hold thereon and pull you to the ground; also

look carefully to yourself at the first, and by
all means shun his blows, making him to toil
and run after, especially there where most dust
is, and spring it up with your feet, make it fly
in his eyes, take your advantage, and smite and
bite him where you may do him most mischief,

ever and anon striking him on the face with
your tail, and that will take from him both
sight and understanding.   Besides, it will so
tire and weary him, that, his feet not being
fully cured of their hurt by the loss of his
shoes, which you caused to be pulled off, he
will no be able to pursue you; for though he
is great, yet his heart is little and weak.

'This, nephew, is mine advice, and assure yourself in these cases art prevaileth as much as courage; therefore regard yourself well, that not only yourself, but your whole family may gain honour and reputation from your

fortune.   As for the charm of prayer which your uncle *Martin* taught me, by which you may be invisible, it is this which followeth': then laying her hand upon his head, she said, '*Blaerd, Shay, Alphenio, Rasbuc, Gorsons, Arsbuntro.* Now, nephew, assure yourself you are free from all mischief or danger whatsoever, therefore go to your rest, for it is near day, and some sleep will make the body better disposed.'

The fox gave her infinite thanks, and told her, 'She had bound him to her a servant for ever; and in those holy words she had spoken he had placed his confidence unremovable'; and so he laid him down to rest under a tree in the grass, till it was sunrise, at which time the otter came unto him and awaked him and gave a fat young duck to eat, saying, 'Dear cousin, I have toiled all this night to get this present for you, which I took from a fowler; here take and eat it, and it shall give you vigour and courage.'

The fox gave him many thanks, and said, 'It was a fortunate handsel, and if he survived that day he should find he would requite it'; so the fox ate the duck without bread or sauce more than his hunger, and to it he drank four great draughts of water, and then he went to the place appointed where the lists stood, with all his kindred attending on him.

When the King beheld *Reynard* thus shorn and oiled, he said to him, 'Well, fox, I see you are careful of your own safety; you respect not beauty so you escape danger.'

The fox answered not a word, but bowing himself down humbly to the earth, both before the King and the Queen's Majesties, went forth into the field; and at the same time the wolf was also ready, and stood boasting, and giving out many proud and vainglorious speeches. The marshals and rulers of the lists were the leopard and the loss. These brought forth a book, on which the wolf swore and maintained his assertion that the fox was a traitor and a murderer, which he would prove on his body, or else be counted a recreant. Then *Reynard* took the book, and swore he lied as a false traitor and a thief, which he would prove on his body, or be accounted a recreant.

When these ceremonies were done, the marshals of the field bade them do their devoir. And then every creature avoided the lists, save Dame *Rukenaw*, who stood by the fox, and bade him remember the words and instructions she had given him, and call to mind how, when he was scarce seven years old, he had then wisdom enough to pass the darkest night without lantern or candle-light, or the help of the moon, when any occasion required him : and that his experience was much greater, and his reputation of wisdom more frequent with his companions; and therefore to work so as he might win the day, which would be an eternal monument to him and his family for ever.

To this the fox answered, 'My best aunt, assure yourself I will do my best, and not forget a tittle of your counsel. I doubt not but my friends shall reap honour and my foes shame by my actions.' To this the ape said amen, and so departed.

CHAPTER XXIV

Of the combat betwixt the Fox *and the* Wolf, *the event, passages, and victory.*

WHEN none but the combatants were in the lists, the wolf went toward the fox with infinite rage and fury, and thinking to take the fox in his forefeet, the fox leaped nimbly from him and the wolf pursued him, so that there began a tedious chase between them, on which their friends gazed. The wolf taking larger strides than the fox often overtook him, and lifting up his feet to strike him, the fox avoided the blow and smote him on the face with his tail, so that the wolf was stricken almost blind, and he was forced to rest while he cleared his eyes ; which advantage when *Reynard* saw, he scratched up the dust with his feet, and threw it in the eyes of the wolf.

This grieved him worse than the former, so that he durst follow him no longer, for the dust

Q

and sand sticking in his eyes smarted so sore, that of force he must rub and wash it away, which *Reynard* seeing, with all the fury he had he ran upon him, and with his teeth gave him three sore wounds on his head, and scoffing said, 'Have I hit you, Mr. Wolf? I will yet hit you better; you have killed many a lamb and many an innocent beast, and would impose the fault upon me, but you shall find the price of your knavery. I am marked to punish thy sins, and I will give thee thy absolution bravely. It is good for thee that thou use patience, for thy evil life is at my mercy. Yet, notwithstanding, if thou wilt kneel down and ask my forgiveness, and confess thyself vanquished, though thou be the worst thing living, yet I will spare thy life, for my pity makes me loath to kill thee.'

These words made *Isegrim* both mad and desperate, so that he knew not how to express his fury, his wounds bled, his eyes smarted, and his whole body was oppressed. So that in the height of his fury he lifted up his foot and struck the fox so great a blow that he felled him to the ground. But *Reynard*, being nimble, quickly rose up again and encountered the wolf, that between them began a dreadful and doubtful combat.

The wolf was exceeding furious, and ten times he leaped to catch *Reynard* fast, but his skin was so slippery and oily he could not hold him. Nay, so wondrous nimble was he in the fight, that when the wolf thought to have him surest, he would shift himself between his legs and under his belly, and every time gave the wolf a bite with his teeth, or a slap on the face with his tail, that the poor wolf found nothing but despair in the conflict, albeit his strength was much the greater.

Thus many wounds and bitings passing on either side, the one expressing cunning, and the other strength, the one fury, the other temperance; in the end the wolf being enraged that the battle had continued so long, for had his feet been sound it had been much shorter, he said to himself, ' I will make an end of this combat, for I know my very weight is able to crush him to pieces; and I lose much of my reputation, to suffer him thus long to contend against me.'

And this said, he struck the fox again so sore a blow on the head with his foot, that he fell down to the ground, and ere he could recover himself and arise, he caught him in his feet and threw him under him, lying upon him in such wise, as if he would have pressed him to death.

Now began the fox to be grievously afraid, and all his friends also, and all *Isegrim's* friends began to shout for joy; but the fox defended himself as well as he could with his claws, lying along, and the wolf could not hurt him with his claws, his feet were so sore, only with his teeth he snatched at him to bite him, which, when the fox saw, he smote the wolf on the head with his fore-claws, so that he tore the skin between his brows and his ears, and one of his eyes hung out of his head, which put the wolf to infinite torment, and he howled out extremely. Then *Isegrim* wiping his face, the fox took advantage thereof, and with his struggling got upon his feet.

At which the wolf was angry, and striking after him, caught the fox in his arms, and held him fast; never was *Reynard* in so great a strait as then, for at that time great was their contention; but anger now made the wolf forget his smart, and griping the fox altogether under him, as *Reynard* was defending himself his hand lighted into *Isegrim's* mouth, so that he was in danger of losing it. Then said the wolf to the fox, ' Now either yield thyself as vanquished, or else certainly I will kill thee; neither thy dust, thy mocks, nor any subtle invention shall now save thee; thou art now left utterly desperate, and my wounds must have their satisfaction.'

When the fox heard this he thought it was a hard election, for both brought his ruin; and suddenly concluding, he said, 'Dear uncle, since fortune commands me, I yield to be your servant, and at your commandments will travel for you to the Holy Land, or any other pilgrimage, or do any service which shall be beneficial to your soul or the souls of your forefathers. I will do for the King or for our holy father the Pope, I will hold of you my lands and revenues, and as I, so shall all the rest of my kindred; so that you shall be a lord of many lords, and none shall dare to move against you.

' Besides, whatsoever I get of pullets, geese, partridges, or plover, flesh or fish, you, your wife, and children shall have the first choice, ere any are eaten by me. I will ever stand by your side, and wheresoever you go, no danger shall come near you; you are strong, and I am subtle; we two joined together, what force can prevail against us? Again, we are so near in

blood, that nature forbids there should be any
enmity between us; I would not have fought
against you had I been sure of victory, but
that you first appealed me, and then you know
of necessity I must do my uttermost. I have
also in this battle been courteous to you, and
not shown my worst violence, as I would on a
stranger, for I know it is the duty of a nephew
to spare his uncle; and this you might well
perceive by my running from you. I tell you,
it was an action much contrary to my nature,
for I might often have hurt you when I
refused, nor are you worse for me, by anything
more than the blemish of your eye, for which
I am sorry, and wished it had not happened;
yet thereby know that you shall reap rather
benefit than loss thereby, for when other beasts
in their sleep shut two windows, you shall shut
but one.

'As for my wife, children, and lineage, they
shall fall down at your feet before you in any
presence; therefore, I humbly desire you, that
you will suffer poor *Reynard* to live. I know
you will kill me, but what will that avail you,
when you shall never live in safety for fear of
revengement of my kindred? Therefore, temperance in any man's wrath is excellent, whereas

rashness is ever the mother of repentance. But, uncle, I know you to be valiant, wise, and discreet, and you rather seek honour, peace, and good fame than blood and revenge.'

Isegrim the wolf said, ' Infinite dissembler, how fain wouldst thou be freed of my servitude? Too well I understand thee, and know that if thou wert safe on thy feet thou wouldst forswear this submission ; but know all the wealth in the world shall not buy out thy ransom, for thee and thy friends I esteem them not, nor believe anything thou hast uttered. Too well I know thee, and am no bird for thy lime bush, chaff cannot deceive me. Oh how wouldst thou triumph if I should believe thee, and say I wanted wit to understand thee ; but thou shalt know I can look both on this side and beyond thee, thy many deceits used upon me have now armed me against thee. Thou sayest thou hast spared me in the battle ; but look upon me, and my wounds will show how falsely thou liest, thou never gavest me a time to breathe in, nor will I now give thee a minute to repent in.'

Now whilst *Isegrim* was thus talking, the fox bethought himself how he might best get free, and thrusting his other hand down he caught the wolf fast by the neck, and he wrung him so extremely hard thereby, that he made him shriek and howl out with the anguish; then the fox drew his other hand out of his mouth, for the wolf was in such wondrous torment that he had much ado to contain himself from swooning; for this torment exceeded above the pain of his eye, and in the

end he fell over and over in a swoon; then presently *Reynard* leaped upon him, and drew him about the lists and dragged him by the legs, and struck, wounded, and bit him in many places, so that all the whole field might take notice thereof.

At this, all *Isegrim's* friends were full of sorrow, and with great weeping and lamentation went to the King, and prayed him to be pleased to appease the combat, and take it into his own hands; which suit the King granted, and then the leopard and the loss, being marshals, entered the lists, and told the fox and the wolf that the King would speak with them, and that the battle should there end, for he would take it into his own hands and determine thereof; as for themselves they had done sufficiently, neither would the King lose either of them. And to the fox they said the whole field gave him the victory.

The fox said, 'I humbly thank them, and what pleaseth my Lord the King to command I am ready to obey, for mine ambition is no further than to be victor; therefore, I beseech you, let my friends come to attend me, that I may proceed by their advice.'

They answered it was reason; so presently came forth Dame *Slopecade* and *Grimbard* her husband, Dame *Rukenaw* with her two sisters *Bitelus* and *Fulromp*, her two sons, and *Malice* her daughter, the field mouse, the weasel, and above an hundred which would not have come if the fox had lost the conquest; for to him that hath honour will ever flock attendants; but to him that is in loss will nothing but contempt follow. Also, the fox came to the

beaver, the otter, and both their wives
Pauntecerrot and *Ordegale*, and the *Ostrole*,
the *Marten*, and the *Fitchews*, the *Ferret*, the
Squirrel, and a world more than I can name,
and all because he was the victor; nay, divers
which before had complained of him, were now
of nearest kindred, and ready to do him all

service. This is the fashion of the world;
he that is rich and in favour can never be
poor or hungry for friendship, every one will
seem to love him, every one will imitate his
fashions.

Then was a solemn feast held, trumpets
were sounded, cornets winded, shawms, and
all instruments warbled, and every one cried,

'Praised be Heaven for this glorious conquest.' *Reynard* thanked them all kindly, and received them with great joy and gladness; then asked their opinions whether he should yield the victory to the King or no; and Dame *Slopecard* said, 'Yea, by all means, cousin, for it stands with your honour, nor may you deny it.' And so, the marshals going before, they went all to the King, guarding the fox on every side, all the trumpets, pipes, and minstrelsy sounding before him.

When *Reynard* came before the King he fell on his knees, and the King bade him stand up, and said to him, '*Reynard*, you may well rejoice, for you have won much honour this day, therefore here I discharge you, and set you free to go whither your own will leads you, for all contestations I take upon myself, and will have it discussed by the wisest of the kingdom as soon as *Isegrim's* wounds shall be cured, at what time I will send for you, and so proceed to judgment.'

'My worthy and dread Lord,' said the fox, 'I am well repaid with anything that shall please you; yet when I came first to your highness's court, there were many malicious persons which sought my life, whom I never injured ; but they thought to overcome me by joining with mine enemies against me, and thinking the wolf had greater favour than I with your Majesty ; this was the ground of their indignation, wherein they showed their simplicity not to alter the end which followed.'

CHAPTER XXV

How the King forgave the Fox all things, and made him the greatest in his Land, and of his noble return home with all his kindred.

THE King said, ' *Reynard*, you are one that owes me homage and fealty, and I hope I shall ever enjoy it; and for your service here I make you one of the lords of my privy council. Take heed you do not anything unworthily, for here I place you in all your power and authority as formerly you were, hoping you will administer justice equally and truly. For as long as you employ your wit unto virtuous actions, so long the court cannot miss you; for you are a star whose lustre exceeds all other, especially in finding out mischiefs and preventing them. Therefore, remember the moral you yourself told me, and be a lover of truth and equity. From henceforth I will be governed by your wisdom, and there shall not breathe that creature in any kingdom which shall do you injury; but I will highly revenge it. This you shall proclaim through all the nation, and be the chief governor in the same, for the office of high bailiff here I freely

bestow upon you, and I know you may reap great honour thereby.'

All *Reynard's* friends and kindred humbly thanked the King; but he told them it was much short of that he intended to do for their sakes, and advised them all to admonish him to be careful of his faith and loyalty. This said Dame *Rukenaw*, 'Believe it, my Lord, we will not fail in that point, neither fear you the contrary; for should he prove otherwise, we would renounce him.'

Then the fox also thanked the King with fair and courteous words, saying, 'My gracious Lord, I am not worthy of these high honours you do me; yet will ever study with my service how to deserve them; nor shall my counsel at any time be wanting.'

And this said, he took his humble leave of the King, and so departed with the rest of his friends and kindred.

Now whilst these passages happened, *Bruin* the bear, *Tibert* the cat, and *Ereswine* and her children, with the rest of their lineage, drew the wolf out of the field and laid him upon soft litters and hay, and covered him all over very warm, and dressed his wounds, which were to the number of five-and-twenty, by the help of many skilful leeches and surgeons. His sickness and weakness was so great that his feeling was lost; but they rubbed and chafed him on the temples and under the eyes, till he leaped out of his swoon, and howled so loud that all were amazed which heard him; but the physicians gave him cordials to drink, and a dormiture or potion to make him sleep; and then comforted his wife, telling her there was no danger or peril of his life. So the court broke up, and every beast returned to his own home.

R

Amongst the rest *Reynard* the fox took his leave of the King and Queen; she desired him not to be long absent from them. To whom he answered, 'That he would be ever ready at their service, as was his bounden duty, and not himself alone, but all his friends and kindred also.'

And so begging license of his Majesty in all solemn manner and with fair speech, he departed from the court.

WITH *Reynard* all his friends and kinsfolks to the number of forty took their leave also of the King, and went away with the fox, who was no little glad that he had sped so well, and stood so far in the King's favour. For now he had power enough to advance whom he pleased, and pull down any that envied his fortune.

After some travel the fox and all his friends came to his borough or castle of *Malepardus*, where every one, in noble and courteous manner, took leave of each other, and *Reynard* did to every one of them great reverence, and thanked them for the love and honour he had received from them, protesting evermore to

remain their faithful servant, and to send them
in all things wherein his life or goods might be
available unto them ; and so shook hands and
departed.

The fox went to Dame *Ermelin* his wife,
who welcomed him with great tenderness.
And to her and her children he related at
large all the wonders which had befallen him
at the court, and missed no tittle or circumstance therein. Then grew they proud
that his fortune was so excellent ; and the
fox spent his days from thenceforth with
his wife and children in great joy and
content.

There are many plays both comic and moral
which figure out things that never were, only
to make use and benefit of the example, that
men may thereby the better shun vice and
pursue virtues. In like manner this book,
though it contain but matter of jest and sport,
yet if he look seriously thereunto, he may haply
find much moral matter and wisdom worthy
his consideration. Goodness or any good men
shall he not find in it disreputed, for all things
are generally spoken, and every man may take
his own part as his conscience shall instruct
him. If any find himself too much oppressed,

let him shake it off with amendment; if any be clear, let him hold on his path and avoid stumbling. And if any take distaste or offence, let him not blame me but the fox, for it is only his language.

NOTES

In the following Notes I have endeavoured to give rough indications of the parallels existing in other branches of the Reynard Cycle, together with references to modern critical investigations where these parallels are discussed. The references to the *Roman de Renard* are to the 'branches' of M. Martin's (Strassburg, 1882-87) edition, and are indicated by *Ren. br.* The German *Reinhart Fuchs* is referred to as *Rein.* I have used the edition of Reissenberger (Halle, 1886). The Flemish verse is indicated by *Reyn.* (edit. Van Helten, Groningen, 1887). The Flemish prose version is, practically, the base of the one before us, and may best be paralleled by Caxton's version (edit. Thoms, Percy Society, 1844).

CHAPTER I

The beginning of the Plea. *Ren. br.* I., *Rein.* combines with the episode of the sick lion. *Reyn.* vv. 33 *seq.* The earliest form occurs in an Italian version, *Rainardo*, published by Teza (Pisa, 1869), Caxton, cc. i.-iii. Goethe i. 1-88.

P. 1. *Sanden*, Caxton, Stade. Other versions do not localise.

P. 2, *Reynard.* For the etymology see Introduction,

p. xi.   The *y* comes from the Flemish, the Middle English form was *Reneward*.

Isegrim.   The original form was *Isengrim* or possibly *Isangrim*, and was current among the Folk before it appeared in literature (see Introduction, p. xviii.).

P. 3.   *House by violence, Ren. br.*, ii. *Rein.* 563-634.   This incident of the adultery of Reynard with the she-wolf forms the central *motif* in the *Roman*, and was developed in the later branches.   It occurs among folk-tales in which at times the she-bear takes the place of the she-wolf, while on other occasions the hare replaces the fox (cf. Sudre, *Sources*, pp. 153-157).   Marie de France (c. 1200) tells the story of a fox and she-bear.

Refused to swear.   Referred to in a few lines, *Ren. br.* I. 37-42 as here, but developed at greater length in *br.* V.; an earlier form in *Rein.*

P. 4.   *Tibert*.   In *Rein.* Diepreht.   As a personal name one of the earliest actors in the Cycle.

Curtois.   In the *Roman* this is applied to the ewe.

P. 5.   *Panther*, derived from the Pancer, in *Rein.* 126, which has probably only an accidental resemblance to the name of the beast.

Kyward, from the Cuvaert of *Reyn.*   In the later editions of Caxton it is misprinted Ruward.   It is the same word with the same meaning as our 'coward.'

CHAPTER II

Continuation of the Plea, see chap. i., Caxton, chap. iv.

P. 8.   *Grimbard* does not occur in *Rein.*, but probably one of the earlier names.

Brock, that is, the badger.

Reynard's sister's son.   This   is   not   an   attempt   at phylogeny, but merely a relic of the original form of the Cycle which dealt with the feud between Isegrim and Reynard, and connected all the other beast actors by ties of relationship with the protagonists.

P. 9. *Fat flitch of bacon.* A reference to an episode contained in *Ren. br.* V.

P. 10. *Malepardus.* In *Ren.* Malpertius. In *Rein.* Übelloch. Probably Maupertius in Champagne.

P. 11. *Chanticleer.* Familiar to us in Chaucer's use of the name in his *Nonne Preestes Tale.* Occurs in *Rein.* as Schantecler. It is, obviously, a French descriptive term for the ' clear singing ' cock.

CHAPTER III

Chanticleer's Plaint. *Ren. br.* II., Caxton, chap. v. For the sources, see Sudre, chap. iv., section 1.

P. 12. *Tantart, Cragant.* In *Reyn.* Cantaert, craiant.

Copple. A diminutive of Coppe of *Reyn.* Grimm compares the English ' copped hen ' (*Rein. Fuchs*, ccxxxviii.) Chaucer calls Chanticleer's wife, Pertelote, whence the Shakespearian name, Partlet (*I. King Henry IV.*, Act iii. sc. 3 ; *Winter's Tale*, Act ii. sc. 3).

P. 14. *Had made peace*, derived from the Æsopic fable of ' Fox, Cock, and Dog ' (see Jacob's *Æsop*, Cranford edition, lix., and note, p. 214).

CHAPTER IV

Continuation of Chanticleer's Plaint (see chap. iii.).

P. 19. *Placebo.* An anthem used in the office for the dead, and beginning with *Ps. Vulg.* cxiv. 9.

P. 20. *Bruin.* In *Rein.* Brune. In *Ren.* Bruns. In

Reyn. Brun. The name is to be referred to the colour of bear-skin.

CHAPTER V

Bruin and the Honeycomb. *Ren. br.* I. 476-605. Caxton, chap. viii. For the source, see Sudre, *loc. cit.* pp. 180-188.

P. 25. *Honeycombs.* Both in Russian and Finnish, one of the popular names of the bear is ' Honey Eater.'

P. 26. *Lanfert.* One of the few names of men given in the story. In *Ren.* it is written Lanfroi.

P. 28. *Head into the cleft.* A similar incident occurs in the *Fables of Bidpai.* See my edition, in the *Bibl. de Carabas,* p. 73, and references, p. lxxi.

P. 36. *Dieu vous garde.* In the old Flemish original it was *Dieu vo saut.*

CHAPTER VI

Embassage of Tibert. *Ren. br.* XV., Caxton, chap. x.

P. 41. *St. Martin's birds.* The learned are not at one as to which birds these are. Some say the crow, some the goose, while others produce evidence of a wren, with long legs, named after St. Martin.

Skilful in augurism. As is well known, the Ancients drew auguries from the side on which certain birds appeared. When starting on a journey the left was considered unlucky, cf. Hopf, *Thierorakel und Orakelthiere* (Stuttgart, 1888).

CHAPTER VII

Continuation of Tibert's Embassage (see chap. vi.).

P. 48. *Jullock.* She was *Bane,* the priest's wife, a little while before (see p. 33).

CHAPTER VIII

Grimbard's Embassage.

P. 52. *Ermelin.* Not named in *Rein.* *Hermeline* in *Ren.*

P. 54. *Reynardine, Rossel.* In *Ren.* there are three sons, Malebranche, Percehaie, and Rousel. In *Reyn.* there are two, named Reinerdin and Rossel. The fox is named the Russet Dog by the Scotch peasantry.

CHAPTER IX

Reynard's Confession. *Ren. br.* VII. This is one of the incidents that have caused the book to be regarded as a satire upon monks, to which some of its popularity in Protestant Germany is due.

P. 56. *Bind his feet to a bell-rope.* Told at length in *Ren. br.* VIII. In some of the medieval Latin fables the wolf sings in church. In two French folk-tales, collected by Bladé, this is turned into pulling the bell-rope, as in the *Reynard*, from which this touch was probably derived (see Sudre, pp. 242-243).

Catch fish. See *infra*, p. 200.

Steal bacon. See *supra*, p. 9, and note. In one of the fables of Babrius, No. 86, repeated in the prose Greek *Æsop*, ed. Halm 31, it is the fox with swollen paunch who cannot escape (cf. Sudre, *loc. cit.* p. 247).

CHAPTER X

Reynard's Condemnation. *Ren. br.* V.

P. 67. *Bellin*, not in *Rein.* *Belin* in *Ren.*

Oleway.   In *Reyn*. Havi.   Clearly not one of the early names.

Bruel.   *Brunel* in *Reyn*., not in *Rein*. or *Ren*.   In *Reineke Vos Alheit*.   Again a late invention.

Baldwin.   In *Rein*. Baldewin.   One of the earliest names of the Cycle.

Bortle.   In *Reyn*. Boore ; in *Ren*. Bruiant.

P. 68. *Partlet*.   See *supra*, note on p. 12.

CHAPTER XI

P. 69. Reynard Arrested.   *Ren. br*. VII.   Not in *Rein*., but well told in *Reyn*.

CHAPTER XII

P. 74. Reynard's Confession.   For occurrences in comparative literature, see chap. xi.   The skill with which Reynard extracts himself from his perilous position is, perhaps, the most characteristic passage in the whole book. Not even Antony before the Roman mob has chosen so deftly the most effective of arguments.

P. 77. *What can the whole world*.   Reynard can quote Scripture for his own purposes.

P. 78. *King Ermerick*.   The great hoard of the Nibelungen, renowned in Teutonic myth.

P. 79. *Elfe*.   In *Reyn*. Waes, a district in Flanders.

P. 80. *Acon*.   Aix-la-Chapelle.   German *Aachen*.

P. 90. *Received the straw*.   In all transfers of real property under Roman and Feudal Law some material object, supposed to be taken from the land, was almost invariably passed as a *stipulation* of surrender, whence the term. The author of *Reynard* makes a delicious use of this practice here to lend plausibility to his hero's deceit.

P. 91. *Hustreloe*, properly *Hulsterio*. A wood between Hulst and Lillo in East Flanders.

Crekenpit. In *Reyn.* Krickepit. This river is unknown to geography. Grimm suggests that it was placed where 'Greek meets Greek'; as Greek was used in Old German for anything strange and woeful.

CHAPTER XIII

P. 95. Reynard Restored. Caxton, chap. xiii.

P. 97. *Tisellin.* In *Rein.* Diezelin. In *Ren.* Ticcelins. Probably one of the original names.

CHAPTER XIV

P. 100. Reynard Shod. Caxton, chap. xix. Of course in the original, Isegrim and his wife have their paws shod to make Reynard's shoes.

P. 102. *Prendesor, Rapiamus.* These names of Church dignitaries are, of course, satirical, and helped towards the popularity of the *Reynard* in Protestant countries. Learned research is inclined to regard them as later additions and not in the original intention.

P. 103. *Used many ceremonies.* There was a prescribed rule for starting on pilgrimages, the pilgrim being blessed by the priest (see Fosbrooke, *British Monachism,* p. 326).

CHAPTER XV

P. 107. The Slaying of Kyward. Caxton, chap. xx. In the *Ren. br.* I., Couart escapes.

P. 115. *Firapell*, i.e. *Fier à poil.*

CHAPTER XVI

P. 118. Caxton, chaps. xxii.-xxiv.

P. 120. *Laprell.* Not in *Rein.* or *Ren.*

P. 122. *Corbaut.* Not in *Rein.* or *Ren.*

Sharpbeak. From the *Reyn.* Scerpenebbe.

CHAPTER XVII

P. 125. Caxton, chap. xxv.

P. 133. *Rossel and Reynardine.* From *Reyn.* In *Ren.* the three sons are named Malebranche, Percehaie, and Rosel, though the latter is called Rousel in one place. This is clear evidence that the Fox's cubs are a later insertion.

CHAPTER XVIII

P. 135. Reynard's Confession. *Ren. br.* VII., Caxton, chap. xxvii.

P. 137. *Goodly bay mare.* This episode is one of the most widely spread of the medieval editions to *Æsop.* It first occurs in Peter Alfonsi's *Disciplina Clericalis*, v. 4. For other references see my edition of Caxton's *Æsop*, where it forms the first of the *Fabulæ extravagantes, loc. cit.* vol. i. p. 252.

P. 140. *The greatest clerks.* Cf. Chaucer, *The Reve's Tale*, A. 4054.

> The greteste clerkes been noght the wysest men,
> As whylom to the wolf thus spak the mare.

And Prof. Skeat's note thereto, who fails, however, to observe that the quotation in this connection proves that Chaucer had before him some form of *The Reynard.* We may have here another trace of the Middle English *Reynard*, of which the only other fragment that remains is that *Of the Vox and of the Wolf.*

P. 141. *He that will live.* Here begins Reynard's *Apologia pro Domo*, the moral of the tone of the book, which is, in its way, a parody on the clerical morals attached to stories like those of the *Gesta Romanorum.*

CHAPTER XIX

P. 146. Reynard's Second Defence. Caxton, chap. xxviii., xxix.

P. 150. *Martin. Rein.* Kunin. Not in *Ren.*, therefore of very late addition.

P. 155. *Cardinal Paregold.* A late and Protestant touch.

CHAPTER XX

P. 160. Rukenaw's Defence. Caxton, chap. xxix., Rukenaw. Not in *Rein.* or *Ren.*

P. 163. *A man and a serpent.* This well - known story is also widely spread among folk-tales. Prof. Krohn has given references to no less than ninety-four parallels of it in his dissertation, *Mann und Fuchs* (Helsingfors, 1891), to which I have added a few others in *Indian Fairy Tales,* pp. 242, 243.   I there contend for the Indian origin of the whole collection of variants.   The earliest form occurs in Petrus Alfonsi, from whom it probably got into the *Reynard*.

P. 169. *Bitelus, Fulromp, Hatanet.*   Only in *Reyn.*, and therefore very late additions.

CHAPTER XXI

P. 172. Caxton, chap. xxii.

P. 173. *Alkarin.*   Quite an imaginary personage. Possibly, I suggest, a confused reminiscence of Alkoran.

P. 174. *Abrion of Trere.*   Equally imaginary, and certainly unknown in the history of the Treves Jewry. Perhaps a 'Portmanteau' word compounded of Abraham and Aaron.

Seth brought out.   The opening scene of the *Legend of the Holy Cross*, when Adam sends Seth to Paradise for some of the Oil of Mercy, instead of which he gets three Seeds of the Tree of Life, which afterwards grew up into the Cross.   See Ashton, *Legendary History of the Cross*, woodcut 1.

P. 176. *Panther.*   Not the panther of ordinary commerce, but an entirely legendary animal, a cross between lion and tiger.

Great India, earthly Paradise.   Smaller India was Abyssinia.   The earthly Paradise is usually placed in medieval maps as an island, at the top, that is at the extreme east of the habitable world.   See Bevan and Phillott, *Medieval Geography*, p. 25, and A. Graf, *Miti Leggende e Superstizioni*, Turin, 1892.

P. 178. *Crampart.*   The Cambuscan of Chaucer's *Squire's Tale*, derived here from the romance of Cleomades by Adeles Le Roi, Poet Laureate, to Henri III., Duke of Brabant, fl. 1250 (see Clouston, *Magical Elements in the Tale*, p. 409).

P. 180. *The horse.* See my Cranford *Æsop*, xxxiii.

P. 181. *Ass and hound.* See Cranford *Æsop*, x.

P. 183. *My father and Tibert.* See Cranford *Æsop*, xxxviii.

P. 184. *History of the wolf.* See Cranford *Æsop*, v.

P. 190. *Liver of a wolf.* This incident is given in *Ren.*, x.

P. 191. *Master Reynard. Master* was applied mainly to qualified physicians.

P. 192. *Give a part.* This is a variant of the fable of 'The Lion's Share,' on which I have commented, *History of the Æsopic Fable*, pp. 74, 166. M. Sudre develops my thesis, *loc. cit.* p. 128 *seq.* It is clear that we have here the original form of the fable with carnivorous fellow huntsman of the lion as against his herbivorous comrades in Phædrus's fable.

CHAPTER XXII

P. 199. *Catch fish with her tail.* See Introduction, pp. xv-xvii, and Krohn's *Bär, Wolf, und Fuchs*, pp. 25, 44. Also Gerber's further references in *Great Russian Animal Tales*, pp. 48, 49. I have given a translation of the earliest literary version from a Hebrew fable by an English Jew in my *Jews of Angevin England*, pp. 170-172. The Scotch Highland peasants tell the tale to explain 'How the bear lost his tail.'

P. 205. *Two buckets.* Told at length in *Ren. br.* IV. M. Sudre, *loc. cit.* pp. 226-236, contends that the story has nothing to do with the Æsopic fable of 'The Fox and the

Goat.'   The Reynard occurs earliest in Petrus Alfonsi, and was probably derived from the East.

P. 212. *Foul dismal hole.*   In *Ren. br.* XIV. the wolf eats his fill and becomes too fat to get out again.

CHAPTER XXIII

P. 215.   Challenge.   Trial by battle was of course the final resource during the Middle Ages in cases like the present, where there was a conflict of evidence.

CHAPTERS XXIV–V

P. 224.   The Combat.   *Ren. br.* VI., Caxton, chap. xxxix.

THE END

Printed by R. & R. CLARK, LIMITED, *Edinburgh.*

THE CRANFORD SERIES.

REYNARD THE FOX. Edited, with Introduction, by JOSEPH JACOBS. Illustrated by FRANK CALDERON. Crown 8vo, gilt, or edges uncut. 6s.

THE FABLES OF ÆSOP. Selected, told anew, and their History traced, by JOSEPH JACOBS, with about 300 Illustrations by RICHARD HEIGHWAY. Crown 8vo, gilt, or edges uncut. 6s.

SATURDAY REVIEW.—"The new *Æsop* is a very pretty book, and in Mr. Heighway we have an illustrator whose gifts and style are congenial. The artist is peculiarly happy in designing headings and tail-pieces. They recall the art of Bewick."
BLACK AND WHITE.—"A gem of a book. . . . We have never seen Æsop so well illustrated, and Mr. Heighway has achieved a triumph."

GULLIVER'S TRAVELS. With Introduction by HENRY CRAIK, C.B., and 103 Illustrations by C. E. BROCK. Crown 8vo, gilt, or edges uncut. 6s.

ATHENÆUM.—"Most excellently illustrated by Mr. C. E. Brock, whose designs show much power of felicitous invention. A valuable introduction by Mr. H. Craik."
PUNCH.—"A splendid new edition of the wonderful *Gulliver's Travels.*"

CORIDON'S SONG, and other Verses. With Illustrations by HUGH THOMSON, and an Introduction by AUSTIN DOBSON. Crown 8vo, gilt, or edges uncut. 6s.

GLOBE.—"Once more grace and humour, technique and character, are present in his work, on which the word delightful may be bestowed without suspicion of exaggeration."
TIMES.—"We are also indebted to Mr. Dobson for a delightful introduction to a very pretty volume of selected and illustrated verse. . . . Mr. Thomson's charming illustrations. They are full of quaint life and spirit."

TALES OF THE PUNJAB, Told by the People. By ANNIE STEEL. Illustrated by J. LOCKWOOD KIPLING, C.I.E., and Notes by R. C. TEMPLE. Crown 8vo, gilt, or edges uncut. 6s.

DAILY NEWS.—"A collection of fascinating folk-tales gathered orally from the mouths of the natives. . . . Mr. J. L. Kipling's spirited and humorous representations of the denizens of the jungle are as delightful as is the letterpress. The Christmas season will not, we think, bring a more attractive gift to children, young and old, or to students of folk-lore, than this volume."
OBSERVER.—"This delightful volume."
DAILY TELEGRAPH.—"Attractive and humorous, and replete with entertainment for both old and young."

SHAKESPEARE'S ENGLAND. By WILLIAM WINTER. New Edition, revised, with 80 Illustrations. Crown 8vo, gilt. 6s.

ST. JAMES'S GAZETTE.—"Such a brilliant piece of impressionism from this American critic—England, and Shakespeare's particular part of it, seen by the American visitor through the glasses of a Shakespeare enthusiasm—deserved to be a success. It is admirably got up, with a great many excellent illustrations."
BLACK AND WHITE.—"Mr. Winter reflects the romance and sentiment of English rural life in a style as fascinating as it is literary."

MACMILLAN AND CO., LONDON.

THE CRANFORD SERIES.

CRANFORD. By Mrs. GASKELL. With Preface by ANNE THACKERAY RITCHIE, and 100 Illustrations by HUGH THOMSON. Crown 8vo, gilt, or edges uncut. 6s.

PALL MALL GAZETTE.—"One is almost tempted to think, as one turns over the pages of this delightful edition, that Mrs. Gaskell must have written *Cranford* with a prophetic eye for Mr. Hugh Thomson as an illustrator. All the characters in the little village society gain by Mr. Thomson's sympathetic delineation."

DAILY NEWS.—"It is no small feat to have added a chapter to *Cranford* which will enhance the pleasure of the reader of that delightful sketch."

DAILY TELEGRAPH.—"Never have Mrs. Gaskell's charming sketches of *Cranford* appeared in daintier guise. . . . *Cranford* can now boast of a preface that is as near perfection as possible."

DAYS WITH SIR ROGER DE COVERLEY. Reprinted from *The Spectator*. With Illustrations by HUGH THOMSON. Crown 8vo, gilt, or edges uncut. 6s.

MORNING POST.—"It is not the first time by many that the worthy knight has afforded subject for the artist's pencil, but he has never received happier treatment. Mr. Thomson's *Cranford* was excellent indeed, but his *Sir Roger de Coverley* is even better. Among the many drawings it is hard to find those that are specially admirable, for the general level of the merit is so high."

DAILY TELEGRAPH.—"Both in paper and type the reprint leaves nothing to be desired, and Mr. Thomson has evidently found the task of illustrating the diversions of the famous old squire extremely congenial to his tastes."

THE VICAR OF WAKEFIELD. By OLIVER GOLDSMITH. A new Edition, with 182 Illustrations by HUGH THOMSON, and a Preface by AUSTIN DOBSON. Second Edition. Crown 8vo, gilt, or edges uncut. 6s.

TIMES.—"We cannot conclude without mentioning an attractive reprint of an old favourite, *The Vicar of Wakefield*, with a preface by Austin Dobson, and illustrations by Hugh Thomson, sufficiently recommended by the congenial pencil of the artist and the congenial pen of the author of the preface."

SATURDAY REVIEW.—"One of the best illustrated *Vicars* we know."

MACMILLAN AND CO., LONDON.

THE CRANFORD SERIES.

COACHING DAYS AND COACHING WAYS. By W.
Outram Tristram. With 214 Illustrations by Hugh Thomson
and Herbert Railton. New Edition. Crown 8vo, gilt, or edges
uncut. 6s.

ATHENÆUM.—"A very pretty reprint is that of Mr. Tristram's *Coaching Days
and Coaching Ways*, with Mr. Thomson's and Mr. Railton's capital illustrations."

GUARDIAN.—"A reprint in a smaller form of a charming book charmingly
illustrated."

OUR VILLAGE. By Mary Russell Mitford. With a
Preface by Anne Thackeray Ritchie, and 100 Illustrations by
Hugh Thomson. Crown 8vo, gilt, or edges uncut. 6s.

TIMES.—"This charm Mr. Hugh Thomson has admirably seized and expressed in
illustrations almost rivalling Caldecott's in their quaint rendering of the humours of English
rural life."

SATURDAY REVIEW.—"The new illustrated edition of Miss Mitford's *Our
Village* is a book to charm the most fastidious of book lovers. *Our Village* is, of course,
a perennial among favourite books, and is likely to charm many a coming generation in
whatever form it takes. A prettier form than this new edition it has not hitherto known.
Mr. Thomson's expressive and humorous art has never been employed with happier results
than in this beautiful little book."

GUARDIAN.—"Mr. Thomson is a prince among book illustrators, and more than
any other has caught the spirit of Caldecott. . . . Whether the reader prefers Miss
Mitford or her biographer he cannot fail to be happy with one or other of them."

HOUSEHOLD STORIES. From the Collection of the Bros.
Grimm. Translated from the German by Lucy Crane, and done
into pictures by Walter Crane. Crown 8vo, gilt, or edges uncut. 6s.

ACADEMY.—"Grimm's tales are ever fresh. . . . Mr. Walter Crane we have always
liked best in black and white. He has here showered upon us a profusion of designs in
his very happiest style. We doubt whether the children have ever had so much pains
taken for them before. . . . The smaller cuts—initials, head and tail pieces—are simply
perfect. Animals and birds, grotesque incidents, and arabesques are Mr. Crane's special
province, in which he has no competitor."

ATHENÆUM.—"It is very readable, and the dialogue is always brisk and life-like.
Her choice, too, fell on some of the best stories in Grimm's collection. What delightful
stories they are!"

SATURDAY REVIEW.—"Mr. Walter Crane has treated these immortal stories
as an old missal painter would have done his breviary or his psalter. Every corner is full
of Mr. Crane's pretty and ingenious fancies. The title-page itself is a study."

MACMILLAN AND CO., LONDON.

THE CRANFORD SERIES.

RIP VAN WINKLE AND THE LEGEND OF SLEEPY HOLLOW. By WASHINGTON IRVING. With 53 Illustrations and a Preface by GEORGE BOUGHTON, A.R.A. Crown 8vo, gilt, or edges uncut. 6s.

TIMES.—" Mr. George Boughton has done justice to the engaging good-for-nothing in a set of fifty-three clever illustrations."

ATHENÆUM.—" The able Academician to whom we owe these excellent illustrations was never, artistically speaking, seen to greater advantage. The comely little volume ought to be welcome."

GLOBE.—" Mr. Boughton's drawings are full of sympathy and charm."

HUMOROUS POEMS. By THOMAS HOOD. With a Preface by ALFRED AINGER, and 130 Illustrations by CHARLES E. BROCK. Crown 8vo, gilt, or edges uncut. 6s.

SATURDAY REVIEW.—" Hood, who was his own illustrator, in more than one sense, has found a new and a successful illustrator in Mr. Charles E. Brock, who contributes something over a hundred vivacious drawings to *Humorous Poems*, by Thomas Hood, with a preface by Canon Ainger, whose sketch of Hood's life and writings is written with excellent taste and discernment."

ATHENÆUM.—" More than five score of capital cuts that are worthy of the delightful verses they illustrate. Mr. Brock draws with great crispness and delicacy of touch."

WESTMINSTER REVIEW.—" Canon Ainger's preface is a delightful piece of work."

OLD CHRISTMAS. From the Sketch-Book of WASHINGTON IRVING. Illustrated by R. CALDECOTT. Third Edition. Crown 8vo, gilt, or edges uncut. 6s.

ATHENÆUM.—" The illustrations are ably and prettily drawn, full of spirit where spirit is required. Graceful figures of ladies and girls abound, and there are many charming touches of gentle satire and pleasant humour. . . . The character sketches of single figures are all first-rate."

MORNING POST.—" Messrs. Macmillan and Co. could not have prepared a more suitable nor a more elegant Christmas offering. . . . The illustrations by R. Caldecott are fully worthy of the matter."

STANDARD.—" We have seldom seen a book in which the illustrator is so entirely *en rapport* with the author. If Mr. Irving had been alive, and could have guided a limner's hand to paint his people just as he conceived them, we could hardly have had better likenesses."

BRACEBRIDGE HALL. From the Sketch-Book of WASHINGTON IRVING. Illustrated by R. CALDECOTT. Third Edition. Crown 8vo, gilt, or edges uncut. 6s.

TIMES.—" A very admirable reproduction is Washington Irving's *Bracebridge Hall*, and this not only for the worth of what the writer has written, but for the very pretty and perfect form in which it has been issued. The illustrations are by Randolph Caldecott, whose pencil has already done such good work with the same author's *Old Christmas*, and very clever they are."

ACADEMY.—" Mr. Caldecott's illustrations to *Bracebridge Hall* are distinguished by the same excellent qualities which justified the success of those which appeared last year in *Old Christmas*. The same rare power of drawing movement, the same quick sense of humour, with now and then a touch of tender grace. The same spirit and swing which attracted and entertained the reader of *Old Christmas* reappear in *Bracebridge Hall*."

MACMILLAN AND CO., LONDON.